HJALMAR SÖDERBERG (1869 ___ __, is one of Sweden's leading writers from the *fin-de-siècle* period. He was the author of four novels which have long been acknowledged as classics of Swedish literature: *Förvillelser* (Aberrations, 1895), *Martin Bircks ungdom* (Martin Birck's Youth, 1901), *Doktor Glas* (1905) and *Den allvarsamma leken* (The Serious Game, 1912). If anything, his reputation as a short-story writer is higher still: the stories selected for this volume illustrate the precision of tone and chiselled prose that have led many to proclaim him the master of form in Swedish letters.

Most of Söderberg's writings contain an explicit current of social and moral criticism, and his novels, notably *Doktor Glas*, caused controversy in their day with their frank exploration of sexual and moral issues. To support himself in his writing career, Söderberg worked as a journalist and literary critic. He later turned to writing philosophical and religious criticism, spending the latter part of his life in Copenhagen.

CARL LOFMARK was formerly Professor of German at St David's University College, Lampeter, University of Wales.

Some other books from Norvik Press

Victoria Benedictsson: *Money* (translated by Sarah Death)

Kerstin Ekman: *Childhood* (translated by Rochelle Wright)

Selma Lagerlöf: *A Manor House Tale* (translated by Peter Graves)

Selma Lagerlöf: *The Löwensköld Ring; Charlotte Löwensköld; Anna Svärd* (translated by Linda Schenck)

Selma Lagerlöf: *Lord Arne's Silver* (translated by Sarah Death)

Selma Lagerlöf: *Nils Holgersson's Wonderful Journey through Sweden* (translated by Peter Graves)

Selma Lagerlöf: *The Phantom Carriage* (translated by Peter Graves)

Hjalmar Söderberg: *Martin Birck's Youth* (translated by Tom Ellett)

August Strindberg: *The People of Hemsö* (translated by Peter Graves)

August Strindberg: *The Red Room* (translated by Peter Graves)

August Strindberg: *Strindberg's One-Act Plays: A Selection: Simoom, Facing Death, The Outlaw, The Bond* (translated by Agnes Broomé, Anna Holmwood, John K Mitchinson, Mathelinda Nabugodi, Anna Tebelius and Nichola Smalley)

August Strindberg: *The Defence of a Madman* (translated by Carol Sanders and Janet Garton)

Elin Wägner: *Penwoman* (translated by Sarah Death)

SHORT STORIES

by

Hjalmar Söderberg

Translated from the Swedish
by Carl Lofmark

Norvik Press
2016

A catalogue record for this book is available from the British Library.
ISBN: 978-1-909408-32-6

First published in 1987 by Norvik Press, University of East Anglia, Norwich NR4 7TJ. Reprinted in 1994.

This revised edition first published in 2009. Reprinted in 2016.

Norvik Press
Department of Scandinavian Studies
University College London
Gower Street
London WC1E 6BT
United Kingdom

Website: www.norvikpress.com
E-mail address: norvik.press@ucl.ac.uk

Managing editors: Elettra Carbone, Sarah Death, Janet Garton, C. Claire Thomson.

Cover illustration: Detail of *Slussen i Stockholm på ett vykort från början av 1900-talet*, postcard, 1900s.

Cover design: Elettra Carbone

Printed in the UK by Lightning Source UK Ltd.

CONTENTS

Introduction..7

The Sketch in Indian Ink.................................. 21
The Dream of Eternity..................................... 23
The Chimney-Sweep's Wife.............................. 27
The Fur Coat... 33
Patriarch Papinianus.. 37
Vox populi.. 41
The Wages of Sin... 44
Drizzle.. 48
The History Teacher.. 51
The Clown.. 54
Killing.. 58
A Dog without a Master................................... 62
The Parson's Cows... 65
Satan, the Major and the Court Chaplain.......... 72
After Dinner... 78
The Sixth Sense.. 86
The Consul-General at the Palace Ball............... 90
The Chinese.. 97
The Burning Town... 103
The Kiss... 107
Archimedes' Point.. 110
Rugg... 113

The Talented Dragon...120
Churchyard Arabesque...136
The Sonata of Errors...141
The Stove that Wasn't Real...151

INTRODUCTION

Carl Lofmark

Hjalmar Söderberg (1869-1941) is scarcely known in this country,* but in Sweden he has a considerable reputation as a prose writer and his works are frequently reprinted in both hardback and paperback. He is the author of numerous stories, articles and reviews, several major novels and plays and some important theological studies. He also wrote some poems, but expressed an early disenchantment with verse, since it has about as much effect upon people's ideas as the Royal Opera, where the baritone can rail against tyranny and still get the Vasa medal. Most popular are his short stories, which began to appear in various Stockholm newspapers and literary magazines in the early 1890s and were reprinted in a series of collections published at intervals throughout his life.

Born and brought up in Stockholm, the city provides the background to most of his stories, while such contemporaries as Fröding, Karlfeldt and Selma Lagerlöf idealized the Swedish countryside; where they look back into history, he looks forward towards our own time. Another famous Stockholmer, the poet Bo Bergman, was his lifelong friend and shared many of his interests: Bergman's famous poem 'Marionetterna' (1903; The Puppets) has been described as 'Hjalmar Söderberg in verse'. Söderberg was a bookish person, attracted especially to the French realists Zola and France and to Danish prose writers such as Andersen, Jacobsen and Bang, as well as Strindberg and Ibsen.

After studying at Uppsala, and then working for a time as a customs official, he became a part-time journalist, writing

---

* See editors' note on page 19.

reviews and a column for *Svenska Dagbladet*: many of the stories in this volume were first published in that newspaper. His best known novels are *Martin Bircks ungdom* (1901; Martin Birck's Youth), *Doktor Glas* (1905; Doctor Glas) and *Den allvarsamma leken* (1912; The Serious Game), all of them set in Stockholm. He quickly became famous, indeed notorious for his attacks on religion and his free, 'immoral' treatment of sexual problems. He was always involved in the public debate of political, social and moral questions. From 1917 on he lived in Copenhagen, where he devoted himself increasingly to theological studies, seeking the historical realities behind the traditions of Moses (*Jahves eld*, 1918; Jehovah's Fire) and Jesus (*Jesus Barabbas*, 1928). The furore that followed publication of his *Jesus Barabbas* encouraged him to treat that subject again in *Den förvandlade Messias* (1932; The Transformed Messiah). In the 1930s Söderberg was one of the first to become alarmed at the rise of totalitarianism in Europe; he collaborated with Torgny Segerstedt, the liberal editor of the Gothenburg newspaper *Göteborgs Handels- och Sjöfartstidning*, and published vigorous attacks on the new ideologies. This campaign brought him back into the mainstream of public affairs; it was said that Hitler put ten years on his life. He died during the German occupation of Denmark in 1941.

Söderberg quickly became famous for a clear, often witty style. An early ambition had been to write 'a clear, cold prose with words like sharp teeth', and he made that dream come true. He combines brevity with power: the shortest of short stories can be full of significance and feeling, while his irony betrays the personal mood of a sceptic who has no time for romantic illusions. Though his medium is fiction, he is determined to avoid all that is false or pretentious; early in his career he declared his aim as a writer: 'to seek after the truth, and to give people what he found or thought he had found of it.' This passion for truth remained with him throughout his life.

His stories still make a strong impression today, because they treat basic questions in an honest way. They are concerned with things that do not change: the inner life of people, the real motives behind their actions, the reasons for cruelty and injustice, the nature of the world and the meaning of life in a modern, urban, post-Christian society. They seldom supply answers – for their author is a true sceptic – but they raise important questions and they provoke thought and reflection.

The question of the meaning of life is raised explicitly in *The Sketch in Indian Ink* and *The Dream of Eternity*. It was a critical question for Söderberg after he had lost the Christian faith in which he had been brought up. Religion was not only a great political and social force in his time, it was also a strong emotional support, which gave people a personal sense of purpose and belonging. When his critical consideration of the Christian teachings left him no honest option but to become a freethinker, Söderberg sustained a real loss; he could find no other emotional home, no other basis for morality and action which might replace it. His sense of loss is movingly expressed in *A Dog without a Master*. A few years before his death Söderberg remarked: 'People have always been so fond of that story because they imagine it is about a dog.'

The sense of purpose and security that comes from knowing the meaning to one's life, however absurd that meaning may be, is recalled in *The Dream of Eternity* as something the narrator had possessed when he was young. But the story shows how he has come to abandon that childish fancy. The same is true in *The Sketch in Indian Ink*, where he disguises his personal emotion by assigning the painful episode to some time in the remote past (made more remote by the technique of the framework story) and by a studied nonchalance of style which treats the matter as no more important than the purchase of a cigar. Now, in the time of the framework story, the narrator has given up thinking about life's meaning. In a religious polemic of 1909 Söderberg wrote: 'What foolish conceit is it that makes people want their life to have a particular meaning, a meaning apart from life itself? A different kind of meaning from the life of a flower, a tree or an animal?'

In *The Dream of Eternity* the narrator is shaken out of his faith in life's meaning and forced to contemplate time and eternity. He first sees time through images of old age and rotting wood and a tale of death, that greedy monster that will devour every one of us when our turn comes. But still more frightening are the sinister horrors of eternity, which come to the narrator when he is alone, at night, in the nightmarish dream of eternity.

Another aspect of time appears in *The Burning Town*. We cannot accept our own non-existence. If I think of the world with myself not in it, I must still assume myself as a spectator of that world. Our mental life depends on a body, and we see from the perspective of a self. Hence the persistence of human belief in a life after death: the self must continue to exist somewhere, somehow. The boy in the story cannot understand the problem, but he rebels instinctively at the absurd idea of a world without himself – that must be one of daddy's jokes.

Many of Söderberg's stories are constructed around the thoughts and feelings of a child, or else the narrator recalls events from his own childhood. He usually affects to be old and no longer troubled by the passions of long ago (though in fact the author was only in his twenties when the first eleven of these stories were published), but his opening words often contain some such phrase as 'in my childhood', 'when I was very young', 'many years ago'. The narrative style also is at times reminiscent of the nursery (as when he says he is going to tell us a story and asks us to pay attention), and many of the stories have something of the fairy tale about them. Critics have pointed out that, despite the 'old man' pose, there is something of the child in Söderberg's narrator: his constant asking of fundamental questions, the keen visual sense and alertness to detail, his interest in the thoughts and feelings of animals, especially dogs, the child's immediate and instinctive capacity for pity and sympathy, his quick sensitivity to any sign of falsehood or injustice.

That sensitivity shows in such stories as *The Chimney-Sweep's Wife* or *The Fur Coat*. These tragic narratives have a realism that makes them immediately credible. The characters are typical, their thoughts – which are all revealed – are entirely in character, their conduct perfectly plausible: the whole course of events rings true. We cannot avoid recognizing that the world of these stories is our own world, their cruelty and injustice are real. The kind of behaviour we call inhuman is in fact only too human. Such stories imply their author's protest against a world order which he has to recognize but cannot with equanimity accept. *The History Teacher* exposes the agony of a man who, because he cannot inspire fear, is exposed to the fiendish but natural cruelty of children; *The Chinese*, where dreamy speculations about the inhabitants of Mars gently hint at the inner strangeness of the alien, shows again the author's sympathy for the man who is different from the others and is consequently made to suffer. In every case it is the inner life of the character that interests Söderberg, he analyses motives, thoughts and feelings and tries to penetrate and understand the personality.

He also seeks to penetrate the inner life of animals. He is interested in the thoughts that pass through the mind of a dog (*Vox populi, Killing, Rugg*); he quite understands the beasts' point of view in *The Parson's Cows*, and in *Killing* he also enters, however briefly, into the life of a bird, a spider and a fox. The fox, who has been 'down town on business', resembles his author's dogs, who also have various matters of their own to attend to; but the dog, in addition to his mundane purposes, has a higher purpose to his life, a religion. That theme is most poignantly expressed in *A Dog without a Master*, but occurs again in Rugg, together with further speculations about the nature and condition of dogs.

The dominant interest in Söderberg's life was religion. Though he always attacked the church and its teachings with great vigour, he denied being irreligious. 'You have never heard of an unmusical person with a lively interest in music, or an unmathematical person with a thorough knowledge of mathematics', he wrote. 'If there is such a thing as a "religious sense", then my lasting interest in religion shows that I have that sense – perhaps in greater measure than the countless people whose religiousness consists in believing what they were told in childhood and have never seriously questioned since.' The absurdity of the Bible's account of God's behaviour is pilloried in *Drizzle*, while religious faith is ridiculed in *The Talented Dragon*. Both stories show not only the folly, but also the cruelty of religion, and God noticeably lacks such human characteristics as sympathy or humour (in the latter story it is the ability to laugh that conclusively proves a man is not a god). Some readers may feel that these two stories go too far in their travesty of divine and human folly and become merely ridiculous; but the beliefs which Söderberg attacks are ridiculous beliefs (a God of mercy whose punishments are endless, whose infinite patience expires by the time of Noah, whose cure for human wickedness has conspicuously failed, who lovingly enjoys the spectacle of his own cruel justice: all these are solidly founded in holy writ). The idea that God amiably discusses problems of justice and world government with the Devil is derived from the 'Prologue in Heaven' of Goethe's *Faust*; in this Söderberg is ahead of Strindberg, who later copied the idea for the prologue to his *Dream Play* of 1902.

The story *Patriarch Papinianus*, which tackles the theme of divine justice, was inspired by the Dreyfus affair, which was becoming a great public issue just at the time of Söderberg's visit to Paris in November 1897. Dreyfus had been convicted of treason in 1894; the Senate Vice-President M. Scheurer-Kestner had in July 1896 received evidence of his innocence and tried to reopen the case, but the General Staff was attempting to suppress the evidence and silence the officer who had found it, while defending the real traitor, Esterhazy, and having documents forged to incriminate Dreyfus. The establishment, including the Church, vilified Dreyfus, but a handful of intellectuals, including Zola and Clemenceau, leapt to his defence, and Söderberg joined them. This story, published in *Svenska Dagbladet* on 5 December 1897, contributed to the lively debate in the Swedish press.

Confronted by an evangelizing major in *Satan, the Major and the Court Chaplain*, the narrator stares deep into his glass of mineral water, watching bubbles rise up like souls of the blessed, and does his best to avoid being saved. The man is a religious fanatic, who takes very seriously his duty of saving souls;

Söderberg is amused, yet at the same time he respects the sincerity of a man who genuinely believes and accepts the practical consequences. Very different is his attitude to the representative of the state church (in this case the court chaplain). Such men saw God as a benign Creator who shared their opinions and interests; they had exercised very great power for many centuries, and their rule had not been a blessing for mankind. He shows them, in *Patriarch Papinianus* and *After Dinner*, using their assumed authority to support the most foolish and outrageous moral principles. Söderberg's most sensational treatment of the type was his novel *Doctor Glas* of 1905, where the calculated murder of a horrid but socially respectable priest is represented as the justified killing of a monster.

What particularly offends Söderberg about the clergyman is his dishonesty, which is practically a requirement of the profession; but dishonesty is a widespread human failing, by no means limited to the clergy. Söderberg is always quick to draw attention to insincerity and pretentiousness, wherever they may occur (for example in such stories as *The Sixth Sense* or *The Consul General at the Palace Ball*), while the common moral pretentions of his time, propagated by a mindless public opinion, are attacked in *Vox populi*, where an 'immoral' (but beautiful) work of art is condemned indignantly by two 'moral' (but ugly) old ladies, ably assisted by all the dogs of the neighbourhood. The story was part of a press controversy over the erection of Per Hasselberg's bronze 'Farfadern' (Grandfather) in Humlegård Park in 1896. Söderberg always expects a frank and unprejudiced openness in moral and political debate and a high degree of integrity in the pursuit of truth, both of which run counter to the entrenched interests of the established church.

Söderberg denied hating the clergy. It is foolish, he said, to hate collectively. And as an atheist he felt no more animosity towards Jesus than a Christian might feel towards Baldur or Osiris. He shows himself very capable of portraying individual representatives of the church sympathetically, in *The Parson's Cows* or *The Sonata of Errors*. Both of these stories show another kind of typical clergyman, kindly, sincere, conscientious, though very limited and conservative in his opinions. There is a generous humour about *The Parson's Cows* which allows human weaknesses and failings to be forgiven; in *The Kiss* even dishonesty, which comes to light as we enquire into the secret thoughts of two young people, appears to be forgiven as a result of the delightful humour with which their episode is treated (though the sceptical reader may doubt whether it is entirely forgiven). Another delightful piece is *Churchyard Arabesque*, written for a volume honouring his friend the writer Henning Berger upon his death in 1924, where, at the same time as creating a memorial to Berger, Söderberg amuses himself at the expense of their common enemy the critic Böök (whom Söderberg had once alluded to as 'Löök', 'onion'). Söderberg is indeed a serious author, but he writes with a lively wit and good humour, and this, especially in the later works, preserves him from becoming gloomy and depressing.

Söderberg's quarrel with the Church arises not from any personal animosity, but from his compelling drive to discover the truth and publish what he finds. His stories are above all concerned with ideas. There is little action, but a good deal of thought and discussion. The stories centred on the Consul-General are essentially discussions on questions of political, social or intellectual interest. The Church's view that suicide is immoral and should be punished had been ridiculed in *Drizzle* (1897); now, in *After Dinner*, the question is treated in the calmer, more rational atmosphere of a debate, though it is a debate that is still charged with emotion. Later, in *The Sonata of Errors* (1925), the debate is not even controversial, but an entirely friendly and constructive exchange of experiences between men who are animated by curiosity, but have no urge to prove themselves right or press their opinions upon others. One of these men is a kindly old priest.

The puzzle that arises in *Archimedes' Point* is one of physics: why can I not move myself forward by pushing myself in the back? The title refers to a legendary saying of the philosopher Archimedes (B.C. 287-212), who discovered the principles of dynamics: 'Give me a point on which to stand and I will move the earth!' But finding a firm point to stand on is easier said than done; and that is true in more fields than physics.

While the manner of reflection on all these ideas may seem appropriate to an elderly narrator, the questions considered are often of the speculative kind that more commonly fascinate us in youth. That is certainly true of the last story in this collection, *The Stove That Wasn't Real*: is the world real, or have I imagined it? There are, in fact, difficulties about arguing that the world exists only in my own imagination. For one thing, it means telling other people that they do not exist, and this tends to be not well received. For another thing, I must be remarkably well-informed, when I consult the encyclopaedia, to have imagined all the information it contains, and I must be a genius when I imagine Handel's *Messiah*. Söderberg's story deals with another aspect of the problem: I may be surprised by things being not as I expected, and that suggests that my subjective idea has been corrected by an independent objective world which is no part of me.

The message of these stories is often a sombre one and their view of human nature is disturbing, yet they are told with a sense of humour which develops with the years. The first of them, taken from the early volume *Historietter*, are thoroughly pessimistic, but later, as in *The Sixth Sense* or *The Talented Dragon*, Söderberg's humour becomes so pervasive and cheerful that an inattentive reader might overlook the story's serious implications. Even in his gloomiest mood, Söderberg has time for fun and witty asides, while his most cheerful stories, like *The Parson's Cows* or *The Kiss*, are darkened at times by a touch of cynicism.

His concern for truth is not optimistic and positive, like that of the eighteenth-century rationalist. He is aware that truth may cause pain and misery. That is recognized already by the boy in *The Dream of Eternity* who blames his friend for being glad to deny the soul's immortality, for reporting what he knows with joy, and not with despair. In his novel *Doctor Glas* Söderberg similarly describes reason as an animal that will at first gladly devour the falsehood and nonsense you throw to it, but has a blind, voracious appetite, and will go on to consume all that you love and care for.

Early in life Söderberg's relentless search for truth had devoured not only the comfort and support of religion, but also the belief in free will. In the early autobiographical novel *Martin Birck's Youth* (1901) he plays with a puppet and imagines its thoughts and feelings: 'When you pull on the thread and he starts to play he thinks to himself, "I am a being with free will, I play just as I want to play and entirely for my own pleasure. Oh what fun it is to play!" But when you stop pulling on the thread he feels tired and says to himself, "I can't be bothered to play any more, the finest thing of all is to hang on a hook on the wall and relax completely."' It is like that with Dr Henck in *The Fur Coat*: although his train of thought gives the impression of a rationally controlled life, his logic leads him to positive plans for the future only while he is wearing the fur coat; without the coat his logic leads just as surely to resignation and the reasoned conviction that he will shortly die.

The most important character in these stories is the narrator. Most of them are told in the first person and presented as personal reminiscences. This narrator, from whose memory the stories are drawn, appears to be a shrewd, honest observer of life, an educated man, now looking back with the detachment of age on events of long ago. His statements are qualified with doubts and reservations ('perhaps', 'in my opinion', 'I thought', 'it seemed', 'who knows?'), and these reveal his scrupulous objectivity; his only concern is to find and tell the truth. This narrator is, as has often been observed, a projection of Söderberg himself. His feeling that life is without purpose seems to have sapped his energy, so that he merely observes and comments on the follies and cruelties of life without feeling any impulse to participate and act. The characters, too, are generally passive, like Henck, or the history teacher, or Fredrik and Magda in *The Chimney Sweep's Wife*, or the apprentices who watch Magda's murder with silent curiosity and do not think to intervene. But the narrator's detachment from the events, his irony, his casual tone, his studied unconcern, mask an intense sensitivity, and while such techniques may protect the author, they do not save the reader from the strong emotions which many of the stories convey.

Söderberg's aim was to write clearly, and it is generally acknowledged that he achieved that aim. Every sentence is clearly intelligible, as with Kafka; and yet, as with Kafka, the meaning of the whole story is sometimes far from clear. The author does not always solve the problems he has raised; questions may be asked, or implied, but they are seldom answered. It then remains to the reader to reflect on the issues for himself. The fascination of such tales as *Rugg*, or *The Chinese*, derives precisely from their open-endedness. They are designed not to inform us, but rather to make us think.

Söderberg's literary work derives from his personal experiences, and Stockholm, the city he knew so well, provides the background to many of his stories. He takes for granted that his readers know its streets and cafés (the Danish critic Georg Brandes once reproached him for making that assumption). *Vox populi* leads us from the Royal Library into Humlegård Park, where Hasselberg's bronze group of a man and naked boy was the newest public scandal; in *The Dream of Eternity* we enter a night-club which is recognizably Berns'. *The Parson's Cows* begins outside the Grand Hotel. We visit the Strömparterre, which lies, with its restaurant and waterfront, east of Norrbro Bridge on Helgeandsholm Island, on which the Parliament house stands. Often we accompany the narrator or main character as he walks through old Stockholm (*The Fur Coat, Satan, The Major and the Court Chaplain, The Consul-General at the Palace Ball* etc.). The town is brought to life with a few well-chosen observations and a handful of street names. This technique is sometimes carried abroad, to Hamburg in *Killing*, and to Paris in *Patriarch Papinianus*, which catches in a most vivid way the whole atmosphere of the city at the time of the Dreyfus affair. Copenhagen, Söderberg's home in later years, provides the background for *Churchyard Arabesque* and *The Sonata of Errors*.

I have attempted to convey the sense and spirit of these stories in easily readable modern English. Any translation, however, is an attempt to achieve the impossible, and my use of contemporary English may obscure the fact that most of these stories belong to the life of nearly a century ago. The reader may be reminded of their real date with a jolt when he encounters, for example, a 'scurfy-headed street urchin' (in *Archimedes' Point*) or when a girl 'draws her skirts tightly round her' (in *The Kiss*). But Söderberg wrote the contemporary language of educated people in his day, and it would have been misleading to represent him in an antiquated style which would sound unnatural.

The stories are here arranged in the order which Söderberg assigned to them in his various collections, and the collections are in their chronological sequence. Thus, the first eleven stories are taken from *Historietter* (1898; Short Stories), and the next four are from *Främlingarna* (1903; The Strangers); *The Consul-General at the Palace Ball* belongs together with these but was first published a year later in the journal *Svea* and was subsequently included, like the five following stories, in Söderberg's next collection, *Det mörknar över vägen* (1907; The Road Grows Dark). *The Talented Dragon* was the title story of the collection *Den talangfulla draken* (1913). *Churchyard Arabesque*, which was Söderberg's contribution to *Boken om Henning Berger*, edited by Artur Möller (1924), and *The Sonata of Errors* (first published in the newspaper *Göteborgs Handels- och Sjöfartstidning*, 24 December 1925) were included in *Resan till Rom* (1929; The Journey to Rome), and *The Stove That Wasn't Real* (from the same newspaper, 22 September 1931), appeared in the posthumous *Sista boken* (The Last Book) of 1942.

The early novel *Martin Birck's Youth* and a selection of the short stories were translated into English by C. W. Stork (New York 1930 and 1935), and *Doctor Glas* was translated by Paul Britten Austin (London 1963, paperback ed. 1970). All these are now out of print. A collection of the stories has been translated into German by Helen Oplatka, Manesse Verlag, Zurich 1976.

Editors' note:

Since this introduction was written, for the first edition in 1987, Hjalmar Söderberg has been the subject of renewed interest in English-speaking countries, helped not least by Margaret Atwood's public expressions of admiration for *Doctor Glas* in particular.

All of Söderberg's major novels are currently available in English: Paul Britten Austin's translation of *Doctor Glas* has been reprinted by Harvill Press with an introduction by Margaret Atwood (2002). *Martin Birck's Youth* is available from Norvik Press in a new translation by Tom Ellett (2004), and *The Serious Game*, translated by Eva Claeson, is published by Marion Boyars (2001). Söderberg's first novel, *Förvillelser* (1895; Aberrations), translated by Neil Smith, will shortly be published by Norvik Press.

THE SKETCH IN INDIAN INK

(*Tuschritningen*, 1897)

One April day many years ago, at the time when I still used to wonder about the meaning of life, I went into a little shop in a back street to buy a cigar. I selected a dark, angular El Zelo, stuffed it into my case, paid for it and prepared to go. But suddenly it occurred to me to show the young girl who worked in the shop, and from whom I often used to buy my cigars, a little sketch in Indian ink which I happened to have in my wallet. A young artist had given it to me, and in my opinion it was beautifully done.

'Look at this,' I said and passed it to her, 'what do you think of it?'

She took it in her hand, interested and curious, and she scrutinized it for a long time very closely. She turned it various ways, and her face took on an expression of strenuous mental activity.

'Well, what does it mean?', she said at last with an enquiring look.

I was rather taken aback.

'It doesn't mean anything special,' I replied. 'It is just a landscape. This is the ground and that is the sky, and this over here is a road... an ordinary road...'

'Yes. I can see that,' she hissed in a rather unfriendly tone: 'but I wanted to know what it *means*.'

I stood there embarrassed and quite at a loss. It had never struck me that it ought to mean something. But her assumption was unshakeable. She had got the idea into her head that the picture must be some sort of puzzle. Why should I have shown it to her otherwise? Finally she put it up against the window to make it transparent. Presumably somebody at some time had shown her a special kind of playing card, which in ordinary light shows a nine of diamonds or a jack of spades, but which, if you hold it up to the light, reveals something indecent.

But her experiment produced no result. She gave me back the drawing, and I prepared to leave. Then the poor girl suddenly went very red in the face and burst out with a sob in her throat:

'Oh. I think it's really nasty of you to make a fool of me like that! I know very well that I am only a poor girl and couldn't afford a proper education, but you don't have to make a fool of me. Can't you tell me what your picture means?'

What was I to say? I would have given a great deal to be able to tell her what it meant: but I could not, because it had no meaning.

*

Ah, well; that was many years ago. I now smoke different cigars and buy them at a different shop, and I have stopped wondering about the meaning of life. But that is not because I have found it.

THE DREAM OF ETERNITY

(Drömmen om evigheten, 1897)

When I was still very young I believed with complete certainty that I had an immortal soul. I considered it a holy and precious gift and I was glad and proud of it.

I used to say to myself: 'This life I am living is a dark, confused dream. One day I shall wake up into another dream which is closer to reality and has a deeper meaning than this one. And out of that dream I shall in turn wake up into a third and then a fourth, and each new dream will be closer to the truth than the one before. And coming closer to the truth in this way constitutes the meaning of life, which is deep and full of sig-nificance.'

And in the joy of knowing that I possessed in my immortal soul a capital which I could not lose by gambling or by getting into debt, I proceeded to lead a dissolute life and squandered like a prince what I owned and what was not my own.

But one evening I was with some of my cronies in a big hall gleaming with gold and electric lamps and with a smell of rot and decay coming up through the floorboards. Two young girls with painted faces and an old woman whose wrinkles had been plastered over were dancing on a stage, accompanied by a wailing band, the raucous applause of men and the noise of breaking glasses. We watched these women, drank heavily and talked about the soul's immortality.

'It is ridiculous to believe,' said one of my friends who was older than me, 'that it would be a blessing to have an immortal soul. Look at that old woman dancing over there, whose head and hands shake whenever she stops for a moment. It is obvious that she is nasty and ugly and thoroughly disgusting and gets more

23

and more so every day. Wouldn't it be preposterous to imagine her having an immortal soul! But it is just the same with you and me and all of us. What a sick joke it would be to give us immortality!'

'What I dislike most about what you have said,' I replied, 'is not that you deny the soul's immortality, but that you take pleasure in denying it. Human beings are like children playing in a garden surrounded by a high wall. From time to time a gate is opened in the wall and one of the children disappears through that gate. The others are then told that he has been led away to another garden which is bigger and lovelier than this one. They listen for a while in silence and then they go on playing among the flowers. Imagine now that one of the boys is more inquisitive than the others and climbs up the wall to see where his friends have gone. And when he comes down again he tells the others what he has seen: outside the gate sits a giant who eats up the children that are led out. And every one of them must be led out through that gate when his time comes. You are that boy, Martin: and I find it quite ludicrous that you report what you think you have seen, not full of despair, but pleased with yourself and glad that you know more than the others.'

'The youngest of those girls is very beautiful,' answered Martin.

'It is terrible to be annihilated, and it is also terrible to be unable to be annihilated,' said another of my friends.

Martin pursued his thoughts further.

'Yes,' he said, 'one ought to be able to find a middle way. Gird up thy loins and set forth to discover the mean proportional between time and eternity. Whoever finds that can establish a new religion, for he will have at his command the finest bait that a fisher of men ever possessed.'

The band played noisily to an end. The gilding of the hall gleamed darker through the tobacco smoke, and up through the floorboards there still came a smell of rotting and decay.

We parted and went our separate ways. I wandered through the streets for a long time: I came upon streets I did not recognize and have never seen since, strangely desolate and empty streets, and their rows of houses seemed to open up to let me through, whichever way I turned, and then to close their ranks again behind my back. I did not know where I was until I found myself standing in front of my own door. It was wide open. I went in through the door and up the stairs. At one of the staircase windows I stopped and looked at the moon: I had not noticed before that there was moonlight that evening.

But I have never before nor since seen such a moon. One could not really say it was shining. It was ash-grey and pale and unnaturally big. I stood for a long time staring at that moon, though I was dreadfully tired and longing to go to sleep.

I lived on the third floor. When I had climbed up two flights of stairs I thanked God there was only one left to go. But when I had reached the top of the third flight it struck me that the landing was not dark, as it always was otherwise, but faintly lit just like the others, where the moon shone in through the staircase windows. But there were only three flights of stairs in the house, apart from the attic stairs; for that reason the top landing was always dark.

'The attic door must be open,' I said to myself. 'The light is coming from the attic stairway. It is careless of the cleaners to leave the attic door open: thieves can get up into the attic.'

But there was no attic door. There was only an ordinary staircase, just like the ones below.

So I had miscounted: I still had one flight of stairs to go.

But when I had climbed up these stairs and stood on the landing, I found it hard to stop myself from crying out aloud. For this landing was not dark either, and here, too, there was no attic door standing open but another staircase leading upwards just as before. And through the staircase window the moon shone in, and it was ash-grey and dull and unnaturally big.

I rushed up the stairs. I could not think any more. I staggered up another flight, and another; I was no longer counting them.

I wanted to scream, I wanted to wake up this bedevilled house and see people around me: but my throat was tight with panic. Suddenly I thought of trying to read the names on the door plates. What sort of people could it be that lived in this tower of Babel?

The moonlight was too weak; I struck a match and held it up close to a brass plate.

I read on it the name of one of my friends, who was dead.

Then the bonds of my tongue were loosed and I screamed. 'Help! Help! Help!'

*

That scream was my salvation, for it woke me up from the terrible dream of eternity.

THE CHIMNEY-SWEEP'S WIFE

(Sotarfrun, 1895)

This is a sad, cruel story. I heard it told more than once in my childhood, and it made me marvel and shudder.

In a side street stands a fine old tradesman's house with a smooth grey facade. A big round-arched gateway without any decoration – well, apart from a date and perhaps a couple of garlands of fruit – leads into a narrow cobbled yard with a black stone well like so many others: the sun never finds its way there. In a corner there is an old linden tree with its branches cut back, its bark blackened and its foliage thinned by the years. It is as old as the house, indeed older, and it is still a favourite spot for the children and the cats of the household.

This was once the home of Wetzmann, the chimney-sweep.

Wetzmann the sweep is said to have been a decent fellow. He had got on in life and collected quite a fortune. He was kind to the poor and harsh towards his apprentices, since that was the custom, and no doubt necessary, and he drank warm toddy in the cellar in the evenings – for he had a rough time at home.

His wife was also harsh towards the apprentices, but she was not kind to the poor or to anyone else either. She had been in service as a maid in Wetzmann's house before she became his second wife. In those days Envy and Lust had been the two deadly sins most dominant in her nature: now their place had been taken by Pride and Anger.

She was a big, powerful woman and was said to have been good-looking in her youth.

The sweep's son Fredrik was delicate and pale. He was born of Wetzmann's first marriage and people said he was like his mother. He had a good brain and a gentle nature and was studying to be a priest. He had just enrolled as a student when he was struck down by a long, serious illness which kept him in bed a whole winter.

In one wing of the house lived a charwoman with her daughter Magda. Was her name really Magda? I don't know, but I always thought of her by that name when as a child I heard the old folk talking about her in the dusk of a winter evening; and I pictured to myself the pale, shy little face of a child, with a mass of fair hair and very red lips. She was fifteen years old and had just been confirmed. Perhaps it was because she had been confirmed that I always assumed she was serious and quiet, like the girls I saw in church on Sundays, and I imagined her always wearing a long, plain, black dress.

In the spring, when the student was convalescing, he would ask the charwoman's daughter to come and sit at his bedside for a while in the afternoons and read to him.

Fru Wetzmann did not approve of this. She was afraid a certain feeling might develop between them. As far as she cared, her stepson could go and fall in love with anybody he liked and get engaged too, it was no concern of hers; but not with a charwoman's daughter! She kept a suspicious eye on Magda, but she had to let the arrangement stand. The invalid needed to be occupied somehow, of course, and the doctor had forbidden him to lie reading as he had weak eyes and was not to strain himself.

So Magda sat at his bedside and read aloud from both religious and secular books; and the student lay feeble and pale, listening to her voice and looking at her too, and he began to feel attracted to her.

She had such red lips.

They were almost the same age – he was no more than seventeen or eighteen years old – and they had often played together as children. Before long they were quite affectionate.

Whenever she could, Fru Wetzmann found some pretext for coming into the sick room to see how things were. The two young people should have noticed this and been on their guard; but one doesn't always do what one should. One day she opened the door silently and cautiously, and this is what she found: Magda had left her chair, which had been placed at some distance from the bed, and she was bending over the pillow with her arms round the young man's neck. And he was half propped up with one elbow pressed into the pillow, caressing her with his thin white hand, and they were kissing fervently. And now and then they whispered a few broken, meaningless words.

The sweep's wife went dark red. But she could not help smiling to herself: hadn't it all turned out exactly as she knew it would? But now she would put a stop to it once and for all. Anger and Pride rose up within her, swelled out and glowed in her cheeks and her eyes, which shone with animation: and who knows – as she stood there silent and unseen watching the two young people who had eyes and ears for nothing but each other – who knows, if perhaps Envy and Lust may not also have crept forth from their secret hiding places and played on their own hidden strings in her soul?

She did not stand there thinking any longer, but strode smartly up to the bed, seized the girl's delicate little wrist in an iron grip, called her something insulting and slung her out through the door with a torrent of the vilest abuse imaginable. And then she swore in the interested presence of all the servants and apprentices a solemn, full-blooded oath that if that young slut had the nerve to cross her threshold just once more her hide would get such a battering that she would never move a muscle for fourteen days.

And nobody doubted that she meant to keep her word.

The invalid did not reproach his stepmother. Every time she entered the room he turned his face to the wall; he didn't want to see her or talk to her after the scene with Magda. But one day he had a private word with his father and said that he couldn't live unless he could have Magda for his bride. The old sweep was surprised and annoyed, but he was afraid to raise serious objections straight away: his son was the only person he really liked and who showed him any affection in return, and he could not face the thought of losing him. So he let the matter rest for the time being and confided the problem to his wife.

*

How can I describe what happened after that? It sounds like a bad dream or a story made up to frighten children when they are naughty, and yet it is true.

They say it happened on a Saturday evening in May.

The house is quiet, and so is the street. Possibly somebody is humming a tune at a kitchen window, or some children may be playing down in the alley... The invalid is alone in his room. He is counting the hours and minutes. It is spring outside. Soon it will be summer. Is he never to rise from his bed again, never again to hear the wind in the trees, never measure his day as he used to, with hours of action and hours of rest? And Magda... If only he did not always see her face with that terrified expression that she had when his stepmother seized her by the wrist! She had nothing to be afraid of really. That evil woman wouldn't seriously dare to do her any harm when she knew he had chosen her for his bride.

He lies there thus dreaming, now awake, now dozing, and lets the pupils of his eyes soak up the beam of sunlight reflected on the white door: and when he closes his eyes he sees a floating archipelago of poison-green islands encompassed by an ink-black sea. And as he dozes the green turns into blue, and the black becomes purple with jagged dark edges, and then it all goes black...

He feels a gentle hand touching his forehead, and he jumps up in the bed.

It is Magda. Magda is standing before him, small and tender and with smiling red lips, and she puts a little bunch of wild flowers on the bed-cover in front of him: anemones, meadow saxifrage and violets.

Is it true, is it really Magda?

'How did you dare?' he whispers.

'Your stepmother is out,' she replies. 'I saw her leave just now, dressed to go out. I heard she was going to Södermalm, and it's sure to be some time before she gets back. So I slipped up the stairs and into your room.'

And she stays with him for a long time talking of the woods where she has been walking alone listening to the birds and picking wild flowers for him whom she dearly loves. And they kiss as often as they can and they embrace like two little children and both of them are happy, while the hours pass by and the sunbeam on the white door becomes fiery and red and then pale as it fades away.

'I think you had better go,' says Fredrik. 'She might be back soon. What am I to do if she decides to attack you? I am just lying here weak and ill and I shall be giddy if I get out of bed. You had better go.'

'I am not afraid,' says Magda.

For she wants to prove that she really loves him and that she is willing to suffer pain for the sake of her love.

Not until it is getting dark does she kiss him for the last time and creep out of the house. In the yard she stops for a minute and looks up at the window of the room, where he is lying alone on the white bed with her meadow saxifrage and violets on the bedcover. As she turns round to go to her little room in the other wing of the house she finds herself face to face with Fru Wetzmann and she gives a little shriek.

There is nobody in the yard apart from the two of them, nobody at all. There are walls all around, staring down at them in the gathering darkness with their empty black windows, and the old linden tree trembles in its corner.

'You have been up there,' says the sweep's wife.

I always thought as a child that she smiled as she said that, and that her white teeth shone in the dark like the teeth of her husband's apprentices.

'Yes, I have been with him,' Magda may have replied, straight and defiant still in her chalk-white fear.

And then what happened? We don't know for sure, but there was probably a wild chase round the yard. At the foot of the old linden tree the girl tripped and fell. She did not cry out for help for fear that Fredrik might hear her; and who would have helped her anyway? Her mother was away at work. The furious woman was over her; she had got hold of something to hit with – a broom-handle or something of the sort – and she struck time and time again. A few half stifled cries from a throat paralysed by the fear of death, and then no more.

A couple of the apprentices who had just arrived home stood in the dark by the gateway and looked on, but they made no attempt to help the child. Perhaps they didn't dare to; and perhaps they were influenced also by a faint hope of seeing the lady of the house taken away one day in a Black Maria.

Fru Wetzmann went indoors after exercising her rights – for she felt instinctively that she had a natural right to impose her authority wherever she could or wanted to – and stumbled upon something soft on the stairs. She called for a maid and a light, for it was totally dark up there. It was Fredrik. He had heard the faint cries, jumped out of bed and rushed out, and he had fallen on the stairs.

*

Magda lived for three days; then she died and was buried.

Wetzmann the sweep paid a sum of money to her mother, the charwoman, and the matter was settled out of court. But it was still a hard blow for the old man. He stopped going to the cellar to drink toddy and mostly sat in a leather chair trying to read an old Bible. He went into a decline, became strange and quiet, and within the year he too was dead and buried.

His son Fredrik slowly got better; but he never finished his theological studies, for both his concentration and his mental powers had been impaired. He was often seen taking flowers to Magda's grave; he walked very fast, leaning forwards, indeed he almost ran, as if he had a number of urgent errands to attend to, and he usually had some books under his arm, too. Finally he became quite insane.

And the sweep's wife? She seems to have had a robust constitution. There are people who are not exactly devoid of conscience, but who never by themselves come upon the idea that they might have done something wrong. It may happen that a man in a blue uniform with shiny buttons lays a hand on their shoulder and tells them to come along with him. Then conscience awakes. But no one came to Fru Wetzmann. She put her stepson into an institution when he became too difficult at home, and she mourned for her husband as is proper and customary, and then she married again. And on her wedding day she went to the church wearing a lilac satin jacket with gold braid, 'dressed up to the nines' – that is what my grandmother said, who was sitting at her window in the house opposite and saw the whole show as she was turning a page in her book of sermons.

THE FUR COAT

(Pälsen, 1897)

It was a cold winter that year. People shrank in the cold and became smaller, apart from those who had fur coats.

District Judge John Richardt had a big fur coat. This was virtually a necessity in view of his position, for he was managing director of a brand new company. His old friend Dr Henck, on the other hand, did not have a fur coat: instead, he had a beautiful wife and three children. Dr Henck was thin and pale. Some people grow fat as a result of marriage, others grow thin. Dr Henck had grown thin; and Christmas Eve came along.

'This has been a bad year for me,' said Dr Henck to himself as, in the Christmas Eve dusk at three o'clock in the afternoon, he went on his way to his old friend John Richardt to borrow money. 'I have had a very bad year. My health is shaky, if not ruined. My patients on the other hand have perked up, practically the whole lot of them; I hardly ever see them these days. I suppose I shall die soon. My wife thinks so too: I've seen that by looking at her. If that is the case it would be best if it happened before the end of January, when that damned life insurance premium has to be paid.'

When he had reached this point in his train of thought he was at the corner of Regeringsgatan and Hamngatan. And as he was crossing the road to continue down Regeringsgatan he slipped on a smooth sledge-track and fell over, and at that moment a sleigh-cab came along at full speed. The driver swore and the horse instinctively swerved to the side, but Dr Henck nevertheless received a blow on the shoulder from one runner and a screw or bolt or something of the kind caught in his overcoat and ripped a big hole in it. People collected around him. A police constable

33

helped him to his feet, a girl brushed the snow off him, an old lady gesticulated over his torn coat in a way that showed she would have liked to mend it on the spot if she could, a prince of the royal house who happened to be passing picked up his hat and placed it upon his head, and everything was in order again, apart from the coat.

'God, what a sight you are, Gustav!' said Judge Richardt when Henck came up to his office.

'Yes, I have been run over,' said Henck.

'Just like you,' said Richardt, laughing good-humouredly. 'But you can't go home looking like that. You can borrow my fur coat and I will send a boy home to fetch me my overcoat.'

'Thank you,' said Dr Henck.

And after borrowing the hundred crowns he needed, he added:

'We'll see you at dinner, then.'

Richardt was a bachelor and he regularly spent Christmas Eve with the Hencks.

*

On his way home Henck was in a better humour than he had been in for a long time.

'It is because of the fur coat,' he said to himself. 'If I had been sensible I would have got myself a fur coat on credit long ago. It would have given me more self-confidence and made people look up to me. People can't pay such tiny fees to a doctor in a fur coat as they can to a doctor in an ordinary overcoat with torn buttonholes. It's a pity I didn't think of that before. Now it's too late.'

He went a little way through Kungsträdgården. It was dark already, it had started snowing again, and people he knew did not recognize him.

'Anyway, who knows if it is too late?' Henck pursued his thoughts further. 'I am not old yet, and I may have been mistaken about my health. I am as poor as a little church mouse; but so was John Richardt not long ago. My wife has been cold and unfriendly towards me lately. Surely she would start to love me again if I could earn more money and if I wore a fur coat. It seemed to me that she liked John more after he had acquired his fur coat than she did before. She was rather taken with him as a girl too, of course; but he never courted her. Instead, he told her and everybody else that he would never dare to marry on less than ten thousand a year. But I dared; and Ellen was a poor girl and wanted to get married. I don't believe she was so in love with me that I could have seduced her if I had wanted to. But I didn't want to anyway; how could I have dreamed of that kind of love? I haven't thought like that since I was sixteen and saw Faust at the opera for the first time, with Arnoldson.* But I am sure anyway that she was fond of me when we were first married; one can't be wrong about that sort of thing. Why couldn't she be fond of me again?

'When we were first married she used to say nasty things to John every time they met. But then he founded a company and invited us to the theatre at times and bought a fur coat. And in time my wife naturally grew tired of saying nasty things to him.'

*

Henck had a few more errands to see to before dinner. It was half past five by the time he arrived home laden with packages. His left shoulder felt very tender; otherwise there was nothing to remind him of his mishap in the afternoon apart from the fur coat.

'It will be interesting to see my wife's face when she sees me dressed in furs,' Dr Henck thought to himself.

The hall was quite dark. The lamp was never lit except during consulting hours. 'I can hear her in the drawing room now,' thought Dr Henck. 'She is as light on her feet as a little bird. It's funny, but I still get a warm feeling around my heart every time I hear her steps in the next room.'

Dr Henck was proved right in supposing that his wife would

---

* Translator's note: the tenor Carl Oscar Arnoldson sang the lead in Goethe's *Faust* when it was performed at Stockholm in 1862. Dr Henck here refers to the love of Gretchen, who allows Faust to seduce her..

give him a more affectionate reception when he was wearing a fur coat than she otherwise did. She crept up close to him in the darkest corner of the hall, wrapped her arms gently round his neck and kissed him warmly and passionately. Then she burrowed her head into the collar of his fur coat and whispered:

'Gustav hasn't come home yet.'

'Oh yes,' Dr Henck replied in a lightly trembling voice as he caressed her hair with both hands, 'yes, he has come home.'

*

There was a blazing fire in Dr Henck's study. Whisky and water stood on the table.

Judge Richardt was sprawled out in a big leather-clad easy chair smoking a cigar. Dr Henck sat hunched up in a corner of the sofa. The open door led in to the dining room, where Fru Henck and the children were busy lighting up the Christmas tree.

Dinner had been very quiet. Only the children had been chattering and all talking at once and enjoying themselves.

'You're not saying anything, old fellow,' said Richardt. 'Are you sitting there thinking about your torn overcoat?'

'No,' said Henck. 'I'm thinking rather about the fur coat.'

There was silence for some minutes before he went on:

'I am also thinking about something else. I am sitting here thinking that this is the last Christmas we shall celebrate together. I am a doctor and I know that I have not many days left. I am absolutely certain of it now. And therefore I want to thank you for all the kindness you have shown lately to me and to my wife.'

'Oh, you are mistaken,' muttered Richardt, looking away.

'No,' answered Henck, 'I am not mistaken. And I want to thank you also for lending me your fur coat. It gave me the last seconds of happiness that I have known in my life.'

PATRIARCH PAPINIANUS

(Kyrkofadern Papinianus, 1897)*

I was travelling abroad at one time. I saw rivers, hills and mountains which were quite different from ours. I also saw many cities, and among them Paris.

Paris is a lively, attractive place. The men are polite and considerate, apart from the cab-drivers. The women are beautiful and demanding. The Eiffel Tower is three hundred meters high but the screens round the public lavatories are much lower than with us. The buses are like big houses and mostly drawn by three white horses; but one can never travel on them because they are always full of people. One evening I was nearly run over by one of these buses on the boulevard, but at the last moment I scrambled to safety on a traffic island beneath a big electric street lamp. On the same island stood a priest wearing a long black cassock and a low hat with a wide brim: he also had a cotton umbrella under his arm. I could not see his face, as the hat totally over-shadowed it.

'That was lucky, sir,' he said in a friendly voice.

'Yes, monsieur,' I replied.

Like myself, he was standing waiting for a chance to cross over to the opposite pavement. The buses and cabs drove past in an unbroken file that seemed as if it would never end, and all around us the newsboys cried out so that their poor lungs seemed to crack:

'La Presse! V'la la Presse!'

While I was waiting I dropped the stub of my cigarette and opened my case to light a new one. For I had been standing there smoking a cigarette, and when I considered it was finished I threw it away. But at once a pale-faced little boy, grey with dirt, came out from between the wheels of the buses, where he seemed at home like the fox in the woodland thickets, picked up the cigarette end, put it into his mouth and lit it. And, a shade happier and more cheerful than before, he continued down the boulevard with the cigarette end in his mouth and his newspapers under his arm, shouting:

'V'la la Presse! New development in the Dreyfus affair; Scheurer-Kestner has been making love to a negress! Voilà la Pre-e-esse!'

'Do you not think it strange, sir,' I asked the cleric, 'that M. Scheurer-Kestner's taste for negresses (whether it is true or fabricated) is regarded as evidence for the guilt of Captain Dreyfus and the innocence of Count Esterhazy?'

'Sir,' the priest answered without hesitation, 'superficially it does indeed appear extraordinary. But if one looks at this whole question in its proper perspective one must conclude that it is perfectly justified to see a connection between these things. To have made love to a negress is a very grave sin (though not a mortal sin); it indicates a mentality that is wilfully and deliberately inclined towards evil. It cannot be without significance that God gave the black races such a striking resemblance to devils. To love a negress is almost to seek out hell. And if Captain Dreyfus's defenders are like this, then imagine what sort of person he himself must be!'

'But surely, sir, Captain Dreyfus has not been condemned and deported for his or his friends' bad character in general, but for a quite specific crime; and if he did not commit that crime...'

The cleric gesticulated authoritatively with his umbrella. 'Ah, sir,' he interrupted me, 'the point you are making is not so substantial as you think. Judges are human and are liable to err. In all probability many people are erroneously found guilty; but it is fortunate that we generally remain in ignorance of such cases, and it is both foolish and criminal to wish to bring them to the attention of the public and to attempt to reverse a verdict which has once been arrived at through the proper processes of the law. It is foolish and criminal to wish, for the sake of one individual, to undermine public confidence in the administration of justice and thereby bring society one step nearer to its dissolution. If Captain Dreyfus were really a patriot he would see that for himself. As things stand at present, he cannot serve his country better than by declaring himself guilty. By insisting upon his innocence he is com-mitting that very act of treason against his country of which in the first place he may have been innocent. But it is starting to rain, sir, and you have no umbrella. Perhaps we are going the same way.'

The priest benevolently put up his umbrella above my head and we proceeded into the crowds on the narrow Rue du Faubourg Montmartre.

'What you have said seems to imply, sir,' I began again after collecting my thoughts for a minute, 'that you regard a man's fate in this life, the earthly life, as a matter of altogether inferior importance. But if, then, as I suppose, you see things from the point of view of eternity, is not the good or ill of a nation, from that point of view, just as unimportant as that of the individual?'

'That is impious talk, sir. It is not permitted for a man to regard temporal things from the point of view of eternity. That perspective is reserved exclusively for the Almighty.'

'But... you do not see the fate of Captain Dreyfus from that point of view, then?'

'Not at all.'

'But, sir: when you regard the justice or injustice of his conviction as a matter of inferior importance, do you not all the time have in mind the divine justice which in a future life will make good the wrongs of human justice?'

The priest stopped and looked thoughtfully at his heavy shoes, on which the rain dripped down from his umbrella. His face was now sharply exposed by the gas lighting in a shop window. He had genial and coarse-hewn features. His expression was that of a mathematician or a chess-player pondering over a difficult problem.

'That is not necessarily the case,' he finally replied. 'On that point I am most inclined to follow the opinion which was ex-pressed long ago by the patriarch Papinianus. He considered that it would undermine respect for human justice unduly if one were to teach that it could be corrected by divine justice. The latter has, according to Papinianus, delegated all its powers to the former. He therefore considered it necessary and good that a man who here on earth has been condemned to death unjustly, but with all the legal proprieties observed, must in the life to come remain condemned.'

When the cleric had said this the pensive expression disappeared from his face. 'Good night, sir,' he said in the old genial, friendly voice and he vanished into the steep, narrow street of Notre Dame de Lorette.

VOX POPULI

(*Vox populi*, 1897)

Stockholm is the most moral city in the world. When it chances from time to time that a poet or an artist, in the grip of his inspiration, oversteps the limits of decency and thereby misuses the gifts which Providence gave him, then not only the people but even the little dogs are filled with moral indignation.

I observed that once again yesterday.

As the clock struck three I came out of the Library, worn out by the toil of my researches within its cool walls and heavily laden with books fatter than I shall ever be and so learned that you would not even understand the titles if I told you what they were.

It was a warm, idyllic summer day. I stepped out into the park and turned to walk along a side path under the big green trees. And I came by chance to the little hill where 'Grandfather' sits dreaming motionless and silent while the boy sleeps on his knee.

I collapsed on to the bench in front of the bronze group quite exhausted, threw the books to left and right of me, lit a cigarette and half closed my eyes. I have noticed that you get a more synthetic view of the world when you look at it with half-closed eyes; all the lines become sharper and simpler, all the irrelevant, confusing little nuances merge, the figures glide back and forth across the stage like silhouettes, some nearer, some further away. And I was fortunate indeed to be sitting with half-closed eyes just at that moment, when two frightfully ugly old ladies went by with a little black dog on a lead.

The situation, then, is this: in the background sits Grandfather dreaming his old dream about the generations to come, of which he – no doubt mistakenly, I fear – is thinking something very beautiful; I am sitting in the auditorium; and at the front of the stage, between us, two frightfully ugly old ladies glide on stage, from right to left, with a little black dog on a lead.

As is well known, Grandfather is a highly indecent piece of sculpture – I have to remind you of that in case anyone may have forgotten; for that is part of the story.

The two old ladies stop in front of the bronze group and exchange their thoughts about the work of art; I cannot hear what they are saying, but I see from the shaking of the heads and from the violent waving of the dark green parasols in the air that they are regarding the matter from the point of view of morality rather than aesthetics, and that their verdict is unfavourable.

Meanwhile the little dog runs here and there, as far as his lead will let him, until at last he realizes that something has claimed his mistresses' attention and should therefore claim his, and that this something is that bronze group there on the grass. Thereupon he sits down like a good dog, pricks up his ears and sniffs the air, and listens to the two frightfully ugly old ladies; and like myself he soon concludes from the shaking of the heads and the wild gesticulations of the dark green parasols, that the bronze group as a whole is the object of their intense disapproval. It is therefore natural and proper that he is immediately seized by an inexorable hatred of that group: otherwise he would not be a good dog.

'Woof!' he says, rushing up to the bronze group with such malevolence that the two old ladies take fright and instantly fall silent. 'Woof, woof, woof!'

Now the pantomime starts to get lively: on the one side the little dog, frothing at the mouth and his eyes sparkling with loyal anger, advances step by step against his new mortal enemy as he barks: – 'Woof, woof, woof!' – on the other side the two pale-faced, thin, black-dressed and frightfully ugly old ladies both pull together at the lead and only inch by inch manage to drag themselves and the dog away, until at last they all disappear out into the wings on the left. 'Woof!' says the little dog once more before he disappears, and with that he is out of the story: but that doesn't mean that the story has come to an end.

We all know that when a little dog barks all the other dogs of the neighbourhood promptly join in. And Humlegård Park is full of cheerful young dogs that roll about on the lawns and pass their days in innocent play and, when oc-casion arises, rush up and say 'wow, wow!' if they are big or 'woof, woof!' if they are small; and the smallest of all say 'yap, yap, yap!'

'We can hear barking,' said all these dogs to each other, 'we must join in.' And they came running up from all directions, from the library fountain, from Linné's statue and all the way from Schéele's hill, and they all stopped in front of Grandfather barking:

'Wow, wow, woof, woof! Yap, yap, yap!'

They are barking still.

THE WAGES OF SIN

(*Syndens lön*, 1897)

This story is about a girl and a pharmacist with a white waistcoat.

She was young and slender, with an air of pine-wood and heather about her. and her skin was bronzed by the sun and slightly freckled. That is what she was like when I knew her. But the pharmacist was a quite ordinary pharmacist. He wore a white waistcoat on Sundays, and this happened on a Sunday. It happened at a place in the country, so far away and remote from all the world that nobody in the district apart from the pharmacist knew that one should wear a white waistcoat on Sundays.

Well, it happened like this. One Sunday morning there was a knock on my door. and when I opened it the pharmacist was standing there in his white waistcoat and he bowed several times. He was most polite and very embarrassed.

'I beg your pardon most humbly,' he said. 'But Miss Erika came with her sisters yesterday while you were away, and she left her poetry book so that you and I should write something in it. Here it is. But I really have no idea what I should write. I wonder if you might possibly...?'

And he bowed again several times.

'I will give some thought to the matter,' I replied in a friendly tone.

I took the book and I wrote in it, for my own contribution, a translation of 'Du bist wie eine Blume' which I had made myself and which I always use on these occasions. Then I started to look through my papers to see if I could possibly find some old verses from my schooldays which might be suitable for the pharmacist. At last I came upon this awful poem:

You have driven my wits to confusion
And I long for your smile, so bright:
But you visit me when I am lonely –
For I dreamed of you last night.

In my dream I was walking beside you
On a path in the fading light,
And I saw in the corner of your eye
A tear-drop, glistening bright.
 I kissed your cheek and I kissed your eye
And I kissed the tear to flight,
But most of all your warm red lips
I kissed in my dream last night.

Dreams are not always so happy!
– But I woke before the light,
And I lay there sad and sleepless
Through the long dark hours of night.

For only my eyes have ever caressed
That gentle cheek that I miss,
And the red lips that I dream of
Have never been mine to kiss.

I showed this poem to the pharmacist and suggested that he could use it if he wanted to. He read it attentively, twice over, and he began to glow with delight.

'Did you really write this yourself?' he asked in the innocence of his heart.

'I am afraid so,' I replied.

He thanked me most warmly for my permission to use the poem, and when he left the room I think we both felt that we should soon be on Christian name terms.

*

That evening the girl's parents gave a little party. There were plenty of young people there. We drank cherry juice on a verandah surrounded by greenery.

I sat looking at the girl.

No, she was not herself. Her eyes were bigger and more restless than usual and her lips were redder. And she could not sit still in her chair.

At times she glanced at me furtively but more often she glanced at the pharmacist. And the pharmacist that evening was as jubilant as a cockerel.

And by the time the punch was served we were on Christian name terms.

*

We young folk went down to the meadow to play games. We threw hoops and played other games, and while we played the sun went down behind the hills and it grew dark.

We had piled up our hoops and staves on the ground and we were now standing in groups whispering and laughing as dusk descended. But the girl came up to me out of the shadows, took me by the arm and led me away behind a barn.

'You must answer me a question,' she said. 'Did the pharmacist really write that poem himself?'

Her voice was quivering, and she tried to look away as she spoke.

'Yes,' I said. 'He wrote it last night. I heard him pacing up and down his room all night long.'

But I felt a sting in my heart the moment I had said this: for I could see that she was a sweet and lovable girl and it was a great sin to deceive her like this.

'Who knows?' I said to myself. 'Who knows? Perhaps it is that sin of which the scripture says that it cannot be forgiven.'

*

The twilight grew darker and it was night, and a star looked down between the trees in the young wood where we were walking two by two.

But I walked alone.

I no longer recall which paths I trod that evening. I left the others and went deeper into the woods.

Deep in the woods I saw among the firs the shining white trunk of a birch tree. And by that tree stood two young people, and they were kissing: and I saw that one of them was the girl with an air of pine-wood and heather about her. But the other was the pharmacist, and he was a quite ordinary pharmacist with a white waistcoat. And he was pressing her tight against the white trunk of the birch tree and kissing her.

And when he had kissed her three times, I went away and wept bitterly.

DRIZZLE

(*Duggregnet*, 1897)

It is autumn again and the days are dark, and the sun is hiding in the gloomiest corner of space for fear that someone might notice how pale and old and worn out she has become lately. But while the wind whistles about the windows and the rain gushes down the drainpipes and a wet dog down in the street howls outside a closed gate, and before the first fire of autumn has burnt down in the grate, I will tell you a story about the drizzle.

Listen.

Once upon a time the good Lord was so filled with wrath over the wickedness of men that he determined to punish them by making them still more wicked. Most of all he would have liked, in his great goodness, to drown the whole lot of them in a new Flood: he still remembered how he had enjoyed the spectacle when all living things had been consumed by the last one. But unfortunately he had once in a weak moment promised Noah that he would never do that again.

And so he said one day to the Devil: 'Listen, my friend. You are not exactly a saint, of course, but you do have some good ideas at times and one can discuss things with you. My human beings are wicked and will not mend their ways. My infinite patience has now come to an end, and I have determined to punish them by making them still more wicked. Indeed, I should like to see them all destroy themselves and each other. It seems to me that, although our interests are generally so very different, we might on this occasion be able to find some common ground. What advice can you give me?'

The Devil reflected, biting the end of his tail. 'Lord,' he said at last, 'your wisdom is as great as your goodness. Statistics prove that the greatest number of crimes is committed in autumn, when the days are dark and the skies are grey and the earth is wrapped in rain and fog.'

The good Lord pondered long over these words.

'I understand,' he said finally. 'Your advice is good, and I will follow it. You have some good talents, my friend, but you should use them better.'

The Devil smiled and gave a swish of his tail, for he was flattered and moved; and then he limped home.

The good Lord, however, said to himself:

'Let there be drizzle for ever more. Let the clouds never disperse, and the fog never lift, the sun never shine again. Let it be misty and grey unto the end of days!'

And it was so.

The umbrella makers and wellington boot manufacturers were pleased at first, but it was not long before the smile turned sour even around their lips. People do not appreciate the importance of good weather until they have had to do without it for a while. Cheerful people became gloomy. Gloomy people became insane and hanged themselves in long rows or collected together to hold prayer meetings. Before long, people stopped working, and there was great distress. The crime rate increased enormously, the prisons were overcrowded and the lunatic asylums only had room for the sane. The population declined, and as people died their homes were deserted. The death penalty was imposed for suicide. But nothing helped.

The human race, whose poets and dreamers had for generations imagined an eternal spring, now faced in its last days an everlasting autumn.

Day by day the desolation increased. Lands were wasted, towns became ruins. The dogs collected in the market places and howled. But in the streets an old man limped from house to house with a bag on his back collecting souls. And every evening he limped back home with his sack full.

One evening, however, he did not limp home. Instead, he went to the gates of heaven and straight on up to the good Lord's throne. There, he stopped and bowed, saying:

'Lord, you have aged of late. We have both aged, and that is because we are having such a miserable time. Lord, it was bad advice I gave you. The sins that interest me require a little sunshine now and then if they are to prosper. You have made a rag-and-bone man of me!'

And with these words he threw his dirty bag down on the steps before God's throne so violently that it burst open and the souls fluttered out. And they were not black, but grey.

'These are the souls of the last men,' said the Devil. 'I am giving them to you, Lord. But take care not to use them if you mean to create a new world.'

*

The wind whistles about the windows and the rain gushes down the drainpipes and that is the end of the story. If you have not understood it then take heart at the thought that the weather will be fine tomorrow.

THE HISTORY TEACHER

(*Historieläraren*, 1894)

In the café. At lunch time.

It is getting dark early; winter darkness. Snow and sleet are coming down, and one bent, black silhouette after another slips past the café's big dark window in the busy lunch-time rush, just as once long ago the fantastic figures in the nursery home-made lantern-show were passed back and forth across a sheet of oiled silk by an invisible hand.

There is so-and-so. How he has aged lately!

There he goes. How much longer will he be able to keep going?

And there she goes... Did she really bother to make herself up to go out on a day like this?

Just now my old history teacher went past, white-haired, frail and bent. I suppose he must have been retired a long time now. How worn out and broken-down he looked! When I saw him slip past the window with his bent legs and his crooked back I felt as if my own body, affected by some mysterious sympathetic force, were ready to go down like a knifeblade sinking into its sheath.

Yes, my old history teacher... What deep awesome respect I felt when as a little boy I came to school for the first time and saw his handsome, friendly snow-white head, for he was white even in those days. And then my surprise and bewilderment, which was mixed with contempt, when I came up several years later into the senior school where he taught and got to know him better. For there was no teacher in the whole school we could play up so recklessly and insolently as him. How did it come about?

Fundamentally, that is how it had always been. He had probably realized right from the start that he was incapable of inspiring fear. And so, by way of compensation, he had wanted to make himself more popular. The method he had chosen was to try to make his lessons as funny and entertaining as possible. He paid just about no attention at all to the syllabus; he told stories, drew pictures of popes and emperors on the board and mimed some of the greatest moments of history. He wanted people to laugh, and they did. His lessons were endless paroxysms of laughter. But it was not his jokes the boys laughed at, for very few of us understood them; it was the man himself. Instead of being our mentor he had become our court fool. In his class you could get away with anything. We picked teazle-heads, took them into the classroom and made his lesson into a pitched battle. And it didn't help when the teacher appealed to us not to throw them at him, whatever we did, because precisely that was the best fun of all, especially if you could get them in his hair. And when one day it got known that the old bachelor intended to get married, we prepared during first break a speech of congratulation in the most appalling Latin containing some thoroughly improper pieces of advice for one entering the married state, and at the beginning of the next history lesson this speech was read out with great solemnity by the form prefect...

Not even with the Greek master, who was deaf and nearly blind; no, not even with a silly little trainee teacher would we have dared to go so far.

But then there was another thing: he had financial problems and time and again unsavoury-looking people came looking for him in the classroom with pressing business. And an unfailing source of amusement was the old teacher's mortal terror each time somebody knocked at the door and the boy who went to open it came back with the inevitable news:

'There is a gentleman outside who would like a word with you, sir.'

And so one day – oh, I remember it like yesterday; it was a November day like today and it got dark early and there was rain and snow – one day it happened, that in one and the same history lesson two such calls came, one shortly after the other. Our joy was indescribable, but the teacher seemed depressed. He made a few attempts to get into his usual joking style, but that day it just wouldn't work. It started to get boring; somebody had to think of something.

Suddenly the form prefect stood up – although this time nobody had heard a knock – and he went and opened the door for a third time. A moment later he came back, perfectly serious:

'There is a gentleman outside who wishes to speak to you, sir.'

Then he turned to us and winked, and we understood the joke at once. The form prefect was a bright fellow, he was the only one of us who could have thought up such an idea.

'For Christ's sake!' cried the teacher, almost in tears, and he ran out into the corridor, his coattails flapping round his legs.

There was nobody there, of course.

But the teacher was white when he came back. He made a vain attempt to continue the anecdote he had just started. But his voice gave out. Shattered, he collapsed into his yellow-stained high-backed chair and wept.

That was the end for the old man. He saw financial ruin ahead, and now this... His world fell apart. There was nothing he could do but cry. And so he cried.

THE CLOWN

(*Gycklaren*, 1898)

Yesterday a familiar face flashed past me in the street. It was pale and had a weary expression, but the features were sharp and distinctive.

I did not know his name. I was sure I had seen him before, perhaps a long time ago, but I couldn't remember when or in what circumstances. His face had aroused my interest, but I couldn't explain why, and I dug through all sorts of old recollections in the junk-room of my memory to try to identify him, but all in vain.

That evening I was at the theatre. There I found him again to my surprise on the stage, playing a supporting rôle. He was only slightly made up, I recognized him at once and looked for his name on the programme. I found it, but it was not known to me. I followed his acting with intense interest. He was playing the part of a pitiful, foolish servant, whom everybody made fun of. The part was as feeble as the play, and he played it in a studied and conventional way; but in certain places his voice took on a sharp, bitter tone which didn't belong to the part.

That bitter tone still echoed in my ears late at night, when I was walking up and down in my room. And with its help I finally managed to dig out the memory that was attached to it. I found that we had been at school together; but he was many years younger than myself. When I was in the top form, he was in one of the bottom ones.

When I was in the top class at school I stood at the window one day towards the end of break. School breaks were always specially depressing for me: I could never get round to doing anything. I knew that I had not mastered my work, but I didn't feel like reading it over. The slight feeling of anxiety I felt regarding the next lesson was always completely overshadowed by a much larger anxiety regarding life altogether, by a nagging premonition that the days to come would be just as empty and meaningless as the days that had gone...

And so I walked up and down with my hands in my pockets unable to do anything, and occasionally I stopped by the window, which was open. As I was standing there, my attention was caught by a remarkable episode that was taking place down below in the playground, just beneath the window. A little boy in one of the bottom classes, a child of about ten or eleven, was lying stretched out on his back with a crowd of other boys around him in a ring. Their faces, most of them anyway, had that expression of mal-icious curiosity that children and ignorant people have not learnt to conceal. A little boy with broad shoulders and prominent cheek-bones, who looked very strong for his age, was standing inside the ring with a whip in his hand.

'You are my slave,' he said to the boy on the ground. 'You are, aren't you? Say: I am your slave!'

'I am your slave,' replied the child without hesitating; one could hear that this was not the first time he had said it.

'Stand up!' commanded the other.

The boy stood up.

'Imitate B., what he looks like when he comes into the classroom.'

B. was a teacher who walked on crutches. The boy took a few steps outside the ring, which opened up to make way for him. Then he went back on to the improvised stage and made with his arms and legs the same movements as a man who is walking on crutches. He played the part very well; the illusion was perfect, and the spectators were pleased, but the little actor stood there looking very serious. He had a pale little face and black clothes, perhaps he had lately lost his father or mother.

'Laugh,' commanded the other with a slight lash of the whip that was in his hand. The boy tried to obey, but it wasn't easy. His laughter sounded artificial to start with, but it wasn't long before he managed to laugh a completely natural laugh, and he turned then towards his 'master' as if it was him he was laughing at. But his master already wanted to get his slave to show off new tricks.

'Say: My father is a filthy creep.' There was delight on all sides.

'Laugh!' – 'Cry!'

The child started to imitate crying, but now too he entered fully into the emotion he was commanded to put on. The tears stuck in his throat, and he started to cry real tears.

'Leave him alone,' said one of the older boys in the ring, 'he really is crying.'

And then the school bell rang.

*

Some days later he ran past me on the way home from school. I noticed that his jacket was undone at the back.

'Wait a minute!' I said, 'your jacket has come undone at the back.'

'No it hasn't,' he said, 'they have cut it open with a penknife.'

'Did they mess up that book for you as well?' I asked.

'Yes, they threw it into the gutter.'

'Why are they so nasty to you?'

'I don't know. They are bigger than I am.'

He didn't know any other reason. But it probably wasn't the only one. There must have been something about him which irritated them. I could see that he wasn't like the others. The exception, the failure to conform, always irritates children and common people. The eccentricities of a schoolboy are punished by the teacher with a kindly admonition or a dry satirical smile; but they are punished by the other boys with kicks and punches and a bloody nose, with a torn jacket, a school cap carefully placed under a drainpipe and one's best book thrown into the gutter.

*

So now he is an actor. That was pretty well a case of

56

predestination. Now he talks to a big audience from the stage. It would be strange if one day he should become famous. I believe he does have the talent. Perhaps then he would gradually make his exception into the paradigm, which other people would have to learn to obey like well-behaved regular verbs.

KILLING

(*Att döda*, 1897)

It is written: Thou shalt not kill.

We all know, of course, that it is sometimes necessary to kill.

But perhaps there is something in the old commandment nonetheless. In spite of the layer of dust which the unending battle of life has in the course of years deposited upon my conscience, it still happens at times that I shudder when I think of some of the murders I have committed. I do not remember them all. And some of them were necessary, and over these I feel no regret.

But among those I have killed from spite or a sudden whim I remember above all a little bird, a spider and a fox.

*

Most children are spiteful. When I was a child I went about for a time with a boy who was even more spiteful than I was. He taught me to shoot with a catapult. When the summer holidays came we went into the woods every day with our catapults; and we could not see a little bird sitting and twittering on a bough without at once putting a stone into the catapult and shooting. But we hardly ever hit the target. Birds, like all other animals, have learnt to be on their guard against human beings and we hardly had time to take aim before the bird disappeared like a speck into the blue. This constant bad luck made us so monstrously spiteful that we finally regarded it as a point of honour for us to kill a little bird, however it might be done. Then it chanced one day – not in the woods, but in the corner of the garden which belonged to the country house where we lived – that we saw in a bush a little chick of a bird that had not yet learnt to fly, but just hopped from branch to branch. Without thinking for a moment, we crept up as close as possible and let fly with our catapults. The little bird fell to the ground, but it was not properly dead. It lay there in the grass with its beak wide open and in the beak its little tongue was moving. The eyes were alive, too. We stood dumbfounded, blood-red with shame, and looked at each other. What were we to do? Should we kill it? And then what should we do with a little dead bird?

'He'll soon die by himself,' said my friend.

'Yes,' I said, 'he can't live for long.'

We felt that neither of us dared to touch him again.

The sun had not gone behind a cloud, and the birds were still singing in the trees. But we crept away without looking at each other and we never played again in that corner of the garden.

*

Why did I kill the spider? It was not out of spite; it was purely impulsive: I killed it because it frightened me.

It was in Hamburg. I was sitting alone in a hotel room reading a book. The electric light fell white and cold over the white pages of my book. I had lit all the lamps in the room. It was quiet around me, no sound except the clock ticking on the ledge of the tiled stove and the rustle of paper as I turned the pages. It was a foggy autumn evening; all the unwholesome vapours of the town entered into my room and poisoned my state of mind. Now and then I looked up from the book and out through the window: the dead, empty Alster lake in the fog, the gas flares on the Lombard Bridge...

Suddenly I felt something touching my hand. It was an enormous spider, hairy and fat, creeping across my hand down into the book I was reading. When he saw me looking at him he started to run. I jumped up from the chair and flung the book away from me, white with dread. But the spider had already managed to run down one of my legs on to the floor; like a ball of thread he rolled across the middle of the room as fast as if his back legs had been on fire. I had to kill him, it seemed like plain self-defence. I picked up the book from the floor, threw it at the spider and crushed him.

Isn't there an old superstition that you should never kill a spider?

I didn't dare touch the book. I have never looked at it since.

I had to see a human face... I went to the doorway and rang for the waiter. When he came I stared at him nonplussed until I managed to improvise: 'Bring me a little whisky.'

*

I killed the fox because I had a gun in my hand when I met him.

It seemed obvious to me that I ought to kill a fox if I met him in the woods with a gun in my hand.

It was in the winter. It snowed every day and every day I went walking in the woods with a worthless old gun and a black dog called Gustav. I did not hunt. Sometimes I shot at fir cones to amuse myself and to please Gustav, who at every shot jumped up and barked loudly with delight over the noise. It didn't frighten him, for he had not yet learnt that a gun is an implement for murder.

One day as it was getting dark I met a little fox. He had been down town on business and was now on his way home with a speckled hen between his teeth. I stood hidden behind a juniper bush and he ran close past me without seeing me. I loaded and fired. Why? That is what one does.

The fox continued a few steps forward as if nothing had happened. Then he stopped with a jolt as if suddenly surprised and dropped the hen. And with a weak, anxious cry he stretched himself out in the snow and died. Gustav, the black dog, who was still almost a puppy, bounded up with wild delight, barking as merrily as could be, and gave him a playful nip in the ear. But the next moment he understood that the strange animal was dead. There came an indescribably shy, bewildered look into his bright black eyes. At last he crept close up to me with his tail drooping and howled softly.

I left the fox lying there and went home, for I was cold.

The next day I went along the same path, for it was my favourite walk. I was whistling to myself as I walked along and gave no thought to what had happened the day before. All of a sudden I stopped in my tracks: on the ground before me lay a dead fox. The crows has been picking at the upturned eye and it was covered with blood.

I stood for a moment and looked at the fox as I listened to the sound of two branches being rubbed together by the wind.

'A living fox is a prettier sight than a dead one,' I said to myself.

And after that I found different paths to walk on.

A DOG WITHOUT A MASTER

(*En herrelös hund*, 1894)

A man died, and when he was dead nobody looked after his black dog. The dog mourned for him long and bitterly. But he did not lie down and die on his master's grave, possibly because he did not know where it was, and possibly also because he was at heart a young, happy dog and considered that life still held something for him.

There are two kinds of dogs: dogs that have a master and dogs that do not. Outwardly the difference is not very great; a masterless dog can be just as fat as the others, even fatter. No, the difference lies elsewhere. Man is, for a dog, the infinite, Providence. A master to obey, to follow, to depend on: that is, so to speak, the meaning of a dog's life. He does not have his master in his thoughts every minute of the day, of course, and he does not always follow closely at his heels; oh no, he runs about intent on business of his own, he sniffs at the corners of houses, makes the acquaintance of other dogs, gets hold of a bone if one comes his way and concerns himself with many things; but the instant his master whistles all this goes out of his doggy mind faster than the whip of Jesus drove the moneylenders out of the Temple. For he knows: one thing is needful. And he forgets his house-corner and his bone and his doggy friends and rushes to his master.

The dog, whose master died and was buried without the dog's knowing where, mourned him for a long time; but as the days went by and nothing happened that might remind him of his master, he forgot him. On the street where his master had lived he could no longer find any trace of his scent. When he played in the grass with another dog it often happened that a whistle cut through the air, and in that instant his friend was gone like the wind. Then he pricked up his ears; but no whistle sounded like his master's. And so he forgot him, and he forgot still more: he forgot that he had ever had a master. He forgot that there had ever been a time when he would have thought it not possible for a dog to live without a master. He became what might be called a dog that has seen better days, but only in an inner sense, because outwardly he got along quite well. He lived as a dog can live: he stole a good meal now and then in the market square and got beaten, and had love affairs, and lay down to sleep when he was tired. He made friends and enemies. One day he gave a thorough beating to a dog that was weaker than himself, and another day he was badly thrashed himself by one that was stronger. Early in the morning he could be seen running along his master's street, where out of habit he still spent most of his time. He would trot straight ahead looking as if he had some important business to attend to, sniff in passing at another dog, but without bothering to follow up the acquaintance, then increase his speed, but all at once sit down to scratch behind his ear with feverish energy. The next moment he would leap up and dash across the street to chase a ginger cat into a cellar window and then, resuming his businesslike manner, continue on his way and disappear round the corner.

Thus his day passed; and one year followed closely on the heels of another, and he grew old without noticing it.

It was a dark, cloudy evening, wet and cold, and there was a shower now and then. The old dog had been down town all day on an expedition. He went up the street slowly, limping a little. He stopped a few times to shake his black coat, which with the years had become flecked with grey around the head and neck. As usual he went and sniffed first to the right, then to the left; and he made a detour into a gateway, and when he came out he had another dog with him. The next moment a third joined them. They were young dogs, and frisky, and they wanted him to play with them; but he was in a bad mood, and it was also starting to rain very heavily. Then a whistle pierced the air, a long, sharp whistle. The old dog looked at the two young ones, but they did not react: it was not one of their masters that was whistling. The old dog without a master pricked up his ears; he felt suddenly so strange. There was another whistle, and the old dog jumped in bewilderment first one way and then the other. It was his master that was whistling, and he had to follow! For the third time somebody whistled, just as sharply and persistently as before. Where is he then, which direction? How did I come to be parted from my master? And when did it happen, yesterday or the day before, or perhaps just a little while ago? And what did my master look like, and what sort of scent did he have, and where is he, where is he? He ran around and sniffed at all the passers-by, but none of them was his master, and none of them wanted to be. Then he turned and ran along the street; at the corner he stopped and looked in all directions. His master was not there. Then he bounded back along the street as fast as he could go; the mud splashed about him and the rain poured off his coat. At every corner he stopped, but nowhere was his master to be found. Then he sat down at a cross-roads and stretched his shaggy head up at the sky and howled.

Have you seen, have you heard a forgotten, masterless dog when he stretches his head up at the sky and howls, howls? The other dogs slink quietly away with their tails between their legs; for they cannot comfort him and they cannot help him.

THE PARSON'S COWS

(*Kyrkoherdens kor*, 1901)

For ten years I had not seen my old friend from student days, Pastor Torelius of Lerkila, when one fine warm summer evening recently we bumped into each other on the pavement outside the Grand Hotel. We had been in the same dining set at Uppsala. I no longer recall exactly what I had been reading for at the time – probably the preliminary exam – but he had been preparing for Finals and he was a very serious young man, except on Saturday evenings. For he had regular habits and he was punctual in all things, including the matter of youthful high spirits. He also had a good brain, and since he was of good, old clerical stock and had more than one bishop, if not as an uncle then at least as a family friend, he had made rapid progress and though he was still a young man he already had quite a good parish. All this had given him an essentially bright, harmonious conception of Christianity, and when I now saw him coming towards me on the pavement with open arms as if it had been hardly a week since we parted outside Taddis' café, I might well have thought from his expression that it was Saturday evening if I had not known that it was Friday.

We sat down at a table under the big awning of the Grand's restaurant and took various refreshments. We came to the end of our old memories of student days sooner than we had really expected, and so we conversed mostly about the present. I learned that he had already re-married and that his second marriage promised to be just as happy as the first would have been, had the Lord so wished. He talked about the pleasures of living in the country, which he would not exchange for anything in the world. He liked his parishioners and he believed they also thought well of him. We also touched upon present-day religious movements and I asked him, among other things, whether he was having a lot of trouble with evangelicals among his parishioners.

'You mean the dissenters?' he said. 'No, I can't say I have much trouble. I must admit, though, that they caused me some concern to start with. It was galling when the archbishop came on his visitation and saw that more people were streaming into the meeting-house than into the church. But I was new to the place, my predecessor had to wear the sack-cloth and ashes, and things have improved since then. There is a more tolerant atmosphere now, and although I can't really say I have any more people in the church than before, at least there are not so many in the meeting-house, thank God! – Well, actually there are special reasons for that...'

He broke off and looked rather mysterious, but I questioned him no further and we sat quietly for a minute. On the pavement before us an occasional thin American walked among the fat Stockholmers, across from the Strömparterre came the last notes of a Viennese song, which left a strange silence after it, and through this silence came the mooing of a cow. It came from one of the skerry boats which had just tied up at the waterfront; a moment later the cow could be heard tramping across the gang-plank, another cow followed, and then we saw a little old peasant go by, leading both cows behind him by a rope.

'Those are fine cows,' said the parson, 'though not as good as mine. I have the fattest and best-looking cows in the whole parish. But you have to see cows in green surroundings to understand them. There is nothing I care for more dearly than my cows – of the things of this world, of course. But for that, too, there are...'

'Special reasons?'

'Precisely. Permit me to tell you the whole story, about the cows and the dissenters and my marriage. It all belongs together.

'It was like this:

'Perhaps you remember that it was very hot last year, especially just before midsummer. One day I took a walk around my property, as usual. I went along the path beside the ditches in the full blaze of the sun, I crossed a meadow where my people were cutting the hay and I came to the pasture where my cows were grazing. You can't imagine how beautiful they looked there among the birch trees! I scratched their heads and talked to them as I always do, to May Rose and Buttercup and White Maid – she is my bell-cow, she has no horns and is milk-white – and to Hercules my bull, who is a combination of strength and gentleness. Bulls are the most good-natured of all animals as long as one doesn't irritate them in the first place. I spoke to all of them and they answered me as well as they could and they mooed after me when I left them. I also talked to a born-again tailor whom I met at the bottom of the hill and who was a great light among those people in my parish who had been saved. I have even heard it said that he used to exorcise devils. Well, he gave me a sweet and sour answer, of course, and then I went on down to the lake. It was shining and still. Actually, it is my regular practice never to bathe before midsummer; but that was only a few days away, and I was perspiring with the heat. I couldn't resist it. In the twinkling of an eye my clothes were off, I jumped into the water and swam out. But it was colder than I had expected, and I did not stay in the water for long.

'As I came out I saw all my cows coming towards me. I called them, and they came nearer, but slowly and cautiously. White Maid in the lead, with Hercules close beside her. When they were about ten or fifteen yards away I suddenly realized by their expression that they did not recognize me, indeed they would not even recognize that I was a human being. And in Hercules' eyes I thought I could see something I had never seen there before. I have to admit that all of a sudden I began to shake with fear. And if you would like to know the meaning of such panic-stricken fear, then place yourself stark naked in front of a dozen great beasts with sharp horns – for I have eleven cows and a bull – with the lake behind you!

'I for my part became half crazy with fear and started to run along the bank. Now the cows came to life! I heard them coming up behind me at a brisk trot. What could I do? I grabbed hold of a bough of a tree, which happened to be fairly low, and pulled myself up. And not too soon, for the whole herd was already round me, and Hercules snorted at me and butted at the tree with his horns. Well, at least I was out of his reach and it was so hot that I didn't catch a chill, though I am usually very sensitive to cold around the stomach. I tried to reason with the animals, but it simply was not possible. White Maid responded only with contempt, May Rose gave me an angry look, and Hercules was quite beside himself. And in a way they were quite right. How could they imagine that this strange white animal that at the sight of them took fright and climbed up a tree, and had no black clothes, no spectacles and no wide-brimmed straw hat, was identical with their good friend and master? He must, of course, be their enemy, or at any rate an alien, ridiculous, improper phenomenon which they ought to attack.

'Fortunately, however, violent emotions seldom last long, at least not among cows. After a while the rich grass at their feet began to attract their attention, and I hid myself as far as possible in the branches of the tree in the hope that they would forget me. The animals began to spread out and I had hopes of escaping – the rough bark was hurting my skin – when I heard the voices of girls, laughing and chattering. The schoolmistress and both daughters of the born-again tailor – all three of them saved, of course – were coming down to the lake with towels to bathe! "Now the very devil is loose!" I thought to myself. I only hoped they would not see me, and I resolved in return to keep my eyes turned towards the land. Well, there wasn't much to look at anyway, apart from the youngest. They were so quick with their movements that I scarcely had time to consider what I should do before the youngest of the girls was standing with one foot in the water and with all her clothes laid neatly and tidily upon a rock. To be honest, I didn't dare turn my head for fear of making the leaves rustle. Well, the girls were soon splashing in the water all three of them, and I sat as quiet as a mouse in my tree. One gets used to all sorts of things; the bark no longer hurt my poor skin as much as it had done, and I started to accept my situation and hope for a happy ending to the story. And so there was in the end, but not exactly the way I had thought.

'The girls came back out of the water, but the schoolmistress happened to go a little further away from the shore, naturally just where my clothes were lying. She came running back to report her find: "There's a man's clothes over there, a man must be bathing right next to us – but where has he gone, he must have swum a long way out!" They put on their clothes with feverish haste, they stood and listened. Nothing could be heard, and nothing was to be seen in the lake. Had he been drowned? And who could it be? They would have to inspect the clothes more carefully. The youngest was the boldest, she went to look and she returned to report: "It's the parson! What if he has drowned?" "What will become of his poor soul?" wondered the schoolmistress. "Oh, be quiet about his soul," retorted the youngest, crossly with a lump in her throat, "I went to confirmation classes with him three years ago and I really liked him, even though he didn't have the true faith. But I don't suppose God is as spiteful as you are."

'All at once they were silent and they stared up into the tree, as if spellbound. Then three screams in chorus, and the next moment they were gone like the wind.

'At last, I came down from the tree and got dressed. I was comparatively calm. And you must admit, I had little more to lose. Never has a poor servant of God found himself quite innocently in such a disastrous situation! It was not long before the tailor arrived with two more of the faithful. They looked pretty black all three, but in the tailor's eyes there shone something of a secret fire. You can imagine that scoundrel's delight at the prospect of exorcising the devil from none other than the lawful custodian of his soul, the parish priest! Fortunately, however, I had already put on my clothes, and with them the dignity which I now so badly needed. Before the tailor had time to open his mouth I told him that I would pay him a visit that afternoon and give him a full explanation, whereupon I took my leave of them with a wave of my hand and went on my way with firm composure.

'In the afternoon I had the good fortune to meet the girl first. I found her by a bush in the garden eating gooseberries. Her father, you see, had a nice cottage with a pleasant garden; with worldly goods, too, he had been blessed, and he had saved up and bought this cottage. I explained everything to her and the sweet child believed me at once. She was the only sensible one among them. First of all she had thought I had gone mad, since I had climbed up into a tree stark naked; but now that she heard me talk and could see that I still had possession of my senses, she believed me at once. She was a simple, unaffected girl, and what had happened did not seem to her nearly so dreadful as I had feared. It is true, as somebody once said, that women are closer to nature than men, and they feel less shame over natural things than we do, even though we always believe the opposite when we are young and do not know them.'

'But what about the tailor?'

'He never believed me. But that, of course, did not prevent him from being flattered when I courted his daughter a few months later. You will have gathered by now that she is the girl who is now my wife. But my father-in-law still believes that I climbed up naked into a tree to watch the girls bathing. For the sake of the family, however, he regards this sin as a very natural and pardonable manifestation of human weakness which I have since thoroughly atoned for. But some of his fellow believers regard his indulgence towards me with surprise and displeasure, and that is why the prayer-meetings, which he and his family conduct, are no longer so well attended as they used to be.'

It was getting late and we prepared to leave. As we parted we shook hands warmly and I wished him all good fortune for the victory of the true church and congratulated him on the happy turn which events had taken for him personally.

'Thank you,' he said. 'I am fortunate already. It is true, of course, that my wife does not have the same kind of education as I have; but her heart is educated. And it also made an impression upon me that she laid out her clothes so neatly, while the others threw theirs all over the place.'

SATAN, THE MAJOR AND THE COURT CHAPLAIN

(*Satan, majoren och hovpredikanten*, 1901)

Our host, the affable Consul General, had just tapped on his glass and prayed us be welcome, to which nobody objected. That is the sort of thing one ought to pray if one wishes one's prayers to be answered. The first tepid stream of bordeaux was sliding down our throats like a gentle caress and being united with two sardines in oil and a small glass of gin to form a strange harmony, a mystical prelude before the expansive grandeur and high flights of the full symphony. Down at the end of the table, where I was sitting, there had not been enough ladies to go round, and so I had on one side a court chaplain and on the other a major. I don't know if he was really a proper major, however, for when we all raised our wine glasses and looked to the centre – to the Consul General – he raised instead a glass of mineral water and the eyes under his stern-looking eyebrows wandered out towards the periphery.

The court chaplain, on the other hand, was a proper court chaplain; and since he knew I was an infidel he did not talk to me about the eternal truths, but about the red wine.

'This is something quite special,' he said. 'I noticed that at once. And for me it is most important that the red wine should be good, for I can't drink anything else.'

And he added in a whisper: 'The stomach is playing up.'

I nodded agreement, rather absent-mindedly. Across the table, between flowers and crystal decanters, I saw a lady's face. Her skin was white and her lips were red. She was watching me as she sipped at her wine; at least that's how it seemed to me. And all the while she kept showing the tip of her little red tongue be-tween her lips and moving it about. It was looking at this that made me thoughtful and absent-minded.

Suddenly the major's voice of command awakened me:

'Are you saved, sir?' he asked.

'Yes,' I replied without thinking; for I guessed that this was the only certain way of getting away from the table without being saved.

The major looked rather baffled. He had not expected that answer; for I do not really look as if I have been saved. He took a drink of water and said no more.

A little string ensemble hidden behind a curtain played a Spanish dance in subdued tones.

The chaplain's head, which seemed to hang loosely on its stalk like a ripe fruit, nodded slowly in time with the music.

'There is a god in that music,' he said.

The major stared deep into his glass of water, like one who sees visions. Suddenly he went pale and pushed the glass away. But the next moment he picked it up again and stared down into it biting his lips together; and then he passed it to me.

'Would you tell me if you can see anything,' he said.

I then in my turn stared into the glass, but I saw nothing apart from bubbles of carbon dioxide rising up like souls that have been saved.

I told him I could not see anything.

'It is the music,' he said. 'Satan is in that music.'

'What is it you can see in your glass, major?' I asked.

'Do you see that lady over there, sitting and putting out her tongue? I can see *her* in the glass. And I see her stark naked!'

'Do you mind if I have another look?' I said.

And I stared very long and intently into the glass of water.

'No,' I said at last, 'I can see nothing at all. Perhaps you should have a glass of wine.' He put a few drops of wine into the glass, but instead of drinking he went on staring down into the liquid, which was now faintly reddish.

'It is gone now,' he said at last.

He took a deep breath and mopped the cold sweat from his brow with his napkin. 'If only she would stop putting out her tongue!'

I looked again at the lady over there between the flowers. The tip of her little red tongue was constantly peeping out between her lips, and she kept looking in our direction while this happened. I really did start to believe that she wanted to lead us into temptation, or at least one of us.

'Oh well, you are probably right,' said the major. 'I may just as well drink wine, since it is plain that Satan is everywhere, in the water too.' And with that he filled his glass to the brim, said '*skål!*' with me, and emptied it in a single draught.

'Yes,' he continued, 'Satan is everywhere. There is no way of evading him, one must take him by the horns and keep him down as well as one can. The other day I had been on guard at the palace and I was on my way home wearing my full dress uniform with my plumes on display. And I tell you I met Satan with every step I took, in fact he went with me all the way. As I was walking up Lejonbacken he whispered to me: "Feiff," he said, "that is the Minister of War just in front of you. He must be too fat to pass through the eye of that needle, you know that very well. You had better go up and have a word with him about his soul. Who knows, you might be sowing the first seed of his salvation." But I realized at once that it was Satan and took care not to do his bidding.'

'Excuse me,' I asked, 'but how could you know that it was Satan that spoke to you like that?'

'Well, I will tell you. I knew in my own mind that I was annoyed with the Minister of War because he had been standing right in front of me throughout the audience so that the king hardly saw me. Now the spirit that was urging me to speak to him began with the fact that he was so fat, and so I realized that it must be the Devil tempting me through my jealousy.'

I found nothing to object to in this. The major went on:

'And then I came down to Norrbro Bridge. There I met two girls – you know the sort... They looked at me as I passed by and showed me their tongues, just like the lady over there. Then I heard Satan speaking to me for the second time: "Feiff," he said, "you must not let slip the chance of speaking to those girls and trying to convert them." And this time Satan spoke so like God himself that I stopped in the middle of Norrbro Bridge and turned round to face the girls, all dressed up as I was. And the girls turned round too, and showed me their tongues. Only a very little bit, of course; not like a street-boy sticking out his tongue, but only a little red tip showing between their lips, just like the lady over there. "Well, Feiff," said Satan, "hadn't you better go up to them then? Are you afraid it might look rather bad? Are you a coward, old Feiff?" I was still hesitating and listening for something that might show me what to do. But then Satan became more cunning than before and said: "You can safely go and talk to those girls, Feiff; there is no need to worry that it might be misinterpreted. Everybody knows you are a serious, religious person; if you wanted to, you could even go and flirt with those girls and people would still think you were trying to convert them." That time he was plain enough, I should think, wouldn't you?'

'Yes,' I said, 'that time he was quite plain. I think I might even have been able to recognize him myself if it had happened to me.'

The major continued:

'I crossed over Gustav Adolf's Square. The sun was shining, and people were looking at me. And Satan whispered to me that at sixty years old I still cut a pretty good figure with my feathers on display. That's the sort of nonsense he talks all the time – I don't take any notice of it. Well, then I came into Arsenalsgatan. And there I met a really decrepit old woman. She bowed to me as deeply as she could and said: "Please, general, give a poor old woman a few coppers for a drink." Without stopping to think or to listen to what Satan might have to say to me I took out a 25-öre coin and gave it to her. I had no sooner handed it over than I realized that this had been one of Satan's deeds. What was it I had done? Consider for yourself: I meet an old woman asking for money. Because the weather is fine and the sun is shining on my uniform and my medals and the old woman calls me "general" though I am really only a major in the reserve, she gets the coin. Have I done a good deed? Far from it. The old woman is sure to spend the money on drink – she said so herself, but I didn't pay attention to that until afterwards. Having the coin will not make her any better or any happier; she will be even worse and more wretched than she was before. "Rubbish!" I hear Satan whispering in my ear, "the old hag has already fallen as low as she can fall anyway, and your little coin won't make a scrap of difference." But I refused to listen to him. I crossed over to the pavement on the other side to see where the old woman would go. She was still standing in the doorway of the Commercial Bank begging. I walked up and down pondering what I ought to do. I couldn't really go up to her and ask for the coin back. But I also couldn't answer for myself if I were to let her go and spend it on drink. What was I to do? I think I walked up and down there for best part of an hour keeping an eye on that old woman. In the end she did move: she went up the street to St James's Square and turned the corner into Trädgårdsgatan; and I followed her. I soon caught up with her and started talking to her about her soul. But she was no more capable of talking than walking properly; she just wanted to get inside a pub. I tried to explain in words she could understand, and I even went so far as to compare the kingdom of heaven with an exceptionally big, bright, splendid pub. But I think she preferred little, dark pubs. I started to get tired of the whole thing, and Satan whispered to me: "Feiff," he said, "leave the old woman alone. A couple of officers are coming along over there and they are laughing at you already." But I persevered with the old woman. The officers came up to me and saluted; I saluted in return, and they did not laugh. "Feiff," said Satan, "you could at least go into a doorway with the old woman; it looks as if you are trying to show off how virtuously you behave and how little you care what people think." But I took no notice of him. Instead, I took the old woman home with me and gave her coffee; and the coffee made her a little more sober so that I was able to talk with her. And now she is in the Salvation Army and she doesn't drink any more, but praises God.'

I listened earnestly as I sipped at my wine. But from the other side I felt the court chaplain prodding me in the arm; and as I turned to him he put his hand in front of his mouth and whispered: 'That fellow's not right in his mind.'

'It depends what one means by "right",' I said. 'But I am quite sure in any case that you are more right-minded.'

The court chaplain looked at me warmly with eyes already clouded by the wine and said:

'I know you and I have different views on some matters. But in the case of the so-called "evangelical" movement we are of the very same mind, are we not?'

'Yes,' I replied, 'I am sure we agree in that case. I don't like evangelicals either. But on the other hand, of course, one has to agree that these so-called evangelicals are the only people in our time who correspond to the first Christians. Are they not, chaplain?'

'Quite so,' he said agreeably, 'Of course, of...'

He broke off suddenly and stared into the air before him. He was a real court chaplain, accustomed to agree with all sorts of things. When he talked with his God he made a quite definite effort to be as accommodating as possible, and if he had met Satan in a doorway he would have tried very hard to make an agreeable impression on him too.

But possibly the conclusion in this case struck him as somewhat dubious. Of course, one can't be sure. It is also possible that he in turn had caught sight of the lady who was showing the tip of her tongue, and that may have been the reason why he suddenly broke off and stared out into space.

AFTER DINNER

(*Efter middagen*, 1903)

The little green room was in semi-darkness between the lounge, which was bright with the electric light, and the dark smoking room, which was lit only by a single green lamp that stood on the open lid of the secretaire. In the lounge a distinguished opera singer was singing 'Quando cadran le foglie'. In the smoking room the host sat with an intimate circle of gentlemen by the secretaire, its bright mahogany surface reflecting the green triangle of the lampshade, showing them his celebrated collection of photographs taken from nature, from which it appeared that nature is at times unnatural. In the little green room a pale gentleman and a lady dressed in red sat whispering in a corner, three old ladies sat on the sofa nodding their heads, and in a gilded armchair there dozed a thin little white-haired professor who had been emeritus for a generation. Through the half-open doors of the balcony the February air blew in, refreshing and yet strangely mild, and in the doorway there stood a young girl in white.

The hostess walked across the room:

'You're not cold, are you?' she said. 'Professor, have you ever in all your years known such weather at the beginning of February?'

'My dear lady,' the old man said as he opened one eye a little (the other eyelid no longer responded), 'I have such a bad memory for weather. I don't remember anything about the weather years ago unless it is part of some special association of ideas. In '48, for example. I remember very well what it was like the day the February revolution broke out – how mild the air seemed, and how the sun was shining on the houses across the street – I was sitting outside a café on the Boulevard des Capucines – '

'Darling, you do make yourself so ridiculous with your indecent photographs,' said the hostess as she stuck a frowning nose into the gentlemen's room. 'Ah, music, music! Is there anything in the world that can be compared with music, professor?'

'I don't know. Well, perhaps – the source from which it comes. The common source that gives rise to that gentleman's lovely song and your husband's nasty photographs.'

The Consul General's wife continued to smile engagingly with her lips, but her eyes stared like the eyes of an idiot. When the professor noticed it he closed the other eye as well.

'Love, madame.'

'The Swedes,' he added, 'have acquired a reputation for loving music and hating ideas. For my part I, alas, am quite unmusical.'

A bald-headed gentleman came in from the hall. He was a prominent politician and a member of the First Chamber.

'What news from the Senate?' asked the hostess.

'Great news, my dear cousin. The world is making such progress that it is a joy to behold. After our resolution today we have reached the point where we can all hang ourselves whenever we like and still get a decent burial. Can you resist the temptation?'

The host came up to the doorway and shook hands with the senator:

'Well, how was the debate? Were there any good points?'

'Not really. The minority rallied behind the slogan: the church grieves. One or two of them were on the point of tears. But the bishop was shaking with fury when he had to expound the church's grief. He has a violent nature, the bishop.'

The three old ladies looked around the room, bewildered and alarmed:

'Is it really possible,' said the one in the middle, 'that the First Chamber is advocating suicide?'

'Oh no, far from it... The Chamber was of course agreed that suicide is always immoral. The minister of justice made that point very strongly.'

'The bishop,' said the old professor, 'seems to lack a sense of history. The idea that the church expresses its grief over suicide by burial in silence is quite unhistorical. At one time the church said to the grieving widow: your husband is in hell; obey me, or you will go there too! That is what the church always said, as long as she could and dared and was allowed to say it. And she would still say that today if it were left to her. But that was in the church's days of power, when she could afford to be honest. Nowadays she has to try to keep up with the times. Yes, yes, it can be hard for us old folk sometimes.'

'Oh, professor,' smiled the hostess sweetly, 'you seem to have kept up to date anyway, in spite of your age.'

'I don't have anything to do,' said the professor, 'and so I have time to think. And if I had been in the Chamber, I think that as a curiosity I would have given them a little speech in defence of suicide.'

The girl in white turned round in surprise:

'As a *curiosity*? Grandfather – do you not always *mean* what you say?'

'Oh yes, my child. But there are opinions which it is best not to express except as curiosities.'

'My dear, dear professor,' the hostess's eyes had once again acquired that staring expression which made the old man close his eyes, 'you surely don't mean that we should all go and kill ourselves?'

'No, lady, *we* should not – at least, *you* should not. I only support those suicides which actually take place. And I consider that the great majority of suicides are relatively good and proper acts. I think suicide is nearly always the best thing that the person concerned can do under the given circumstances, and in most cases it would be far more criminal of him to go on living. You see, nature has taken good care to focus our will on the preservation of our life for as long as it can have the slightest value for ourselves or others, indeed often for much, much longer. And in the end it is surely for the individual himself and nobody else to decide whether he ought to live or die. In old Massilia there was a strange law: anyone who wished to die had to present his reasons to the Senate, and if the Senate considered his grounds sufficient, then they gave him a painless poison – cigué I think it was called. To attempt suicide in any other way carried the death penalty. What business that was of the Senate's I do not understand: but the poison was good. The fact is that only in a very few quite exceptional cases does society or any group of individuals really suffer as a result of somebody's suicide – when people think otherwise, that is because they confuse the sort of conduct which commonly leads to suicide with the act itself, and they make a perhaps quite justified condemnation of the man's way of life into a quite unjustified condemnation of his way of death. It is easy to say: "he should have reformed, he should have started a new life, he should have made good what he did wrong." But that is usually not possible. For a man who has been helping himself from the till and knows he is going to be found out it is quite impossible. It is not possible for him either to feed his family or to pay off his debt by sitting in jail, and when he comes out he will be a burden to his nearest and dearest instead of a support. He is quite right to kill himself, and if he has any decency left that is what he will do. And in a thousand other cases as well that "new life" is just as impossible for him to achieve. The man who wants to die is always sick, it may be in his body, or his mind, or his will or his character. And if the will to die prevails over the will to live then that is because his sickness was a mortal sickness. He then has a right to die. It may even be his duty – his duty towards life and those who live on.'

It was silent in the room. Gradually people had come to realize that the old man was serious. 'Yes,' said the senator, standing with his back to the fire and his hand inside his waistcoat, 'yes, from a purely heathen point of view I admit that I can't find any fault in the professor's line of argument. But the professor is forgetting that we live in a Christian society.'

'There is some reason to doubt that,' replied the professor with a smile that revealed an excellent set of false teeth. 'But I can gladly pretend it is true. And then I shall take the liberty of reminding you that the superstitious horror with which popular religion regards suicide has no foundation whatever either in the Christian religion which Jesus taught or in that which is preached nowadays in our churches. It is founded entirely upon a quite unique and very curious view of religion, which has long since been abandoned by all educated people and by most uneducated people as well – indeed, all but forgotten: that is, the idea that a man's fate in the next life depends most of all upon the more or less proper manner in which he departs this life.'

'Well, isn't that strange,' cried the old ladies on the sofa in chorus, 'but at least it says in the catechism that suicide...'

'Yes,' said the professor, 'it would indeed be useful to have a copy of the catechism to hand. I don't know the Bible by heart; but if there really is any passage in it that expressly condemns suicide, then I expect we will find it quoted in the catechism. Perhaps you have a copy of the catechism in your library, Consul General?'

Our host, the affable Consul General, immediately pressed a button on the wall. A smart servant-girl in a black dress with a white pinafore appeared in the doorway.

'Would you mind going to the bookshop on the corner, Hanna, and buying a copy of Dr Martin Luther's little catechism, please?'

'Hm,' said the old bank manager Israel, who had been the last of all the gentlemen to tear himself away from the Consul General's photographs. 'I am afraid I am not all that well versed in your religion, gentlemen. But I believe I can inform you that Yahweh, at any rate before the beginning of the Christian era, did not regard suicide as a particularly serious crime. At its worst it was foolish. Among all his rules and commandments about everything possible, great and small, which Yahweh gave to my people I cannot remember a single word about suicide, or how a suicide should be buried, or anything of that sort. Presumably he thought it unnecessary. He knew he had given the human race such a love for life that they would not be in any great haste to deprive themselves of it. And it wouldn't have been like Yahweh to want to force a man who had been caught stealing from a till to go on making the earth unclean with his existence. Besides. he didn't have any hell at his disposal. The severest penalty he had was death. For that reason there was no action he could take against suicides.

'But to go on to another point while we are sitting here waiting for Dr Luther's catechism,' the bank manager said as he sat himself down in the corner beside the lady in red and turned to her, 'is it really true that they thank God in your churches when somebody has died? When a breadwinner dies in the prime of life – does the priest then thank God on behalf of the widow and the children, and the congregation?'

'I don't know,' said the red lady. 'I never go to church. And when I have been to funerals I have had more to think about than listening to the priest.'

'Oh yes,' said the girl in white, 'yes, that is true.'

'Oh!... and doesn't that offend the congregation?'

'Only the very few of them that really think about it.'

'How strange! Job was a godly man. The most godly man of his day. He said: "The Lord gave and the Lord has taken away: blessed be the name of the Lord." But I don't think he meant it. And anyway it is a very long way from that to actually thanking the Lord for the blow.'

'But,' said the girl in white, 'really it is on behalf of the dead person and not those left behind that the priest thanks God.'

'Hm... So that's how it is... But then the dead man himself is in the best position to judge whether he has anything to be thankful for.'

In came the maid with the catechism.

'Here you are,' she said, 'but they didn't have Luther's catechism, they only had Mazér's.'

And she handed over a little book, which with its white label on the cover looked just like a note-book. On the label it said 'Mazér's Catechism'.

The professor took it, opened it and looked at it with surprise.

'Yes,' he said after turning over the pages for a while, 'there really is a little Bible text here against suicide. "Do yourself no evil.'''

He sat for a moment as if he were searching for something in his memory.

'No, it isn't possible,' he finally burst out. 'It is splendid! It is almost too much! But Mazér isn't to blame; I remember very well – we had that text in the same place when I was a child. Do you know the context, gentlemen? Those are St Paul's words to his gaoler Silas, when he was in prison at Philippi. When the gaoler woke him up he happened to see the door standing ajar – it was surely an angel that had opened it – and so he thought, of course, that the prisoners had escaped. The man was ready to kill himself in despair, but then Paul says: "Do yourself no evil, for all of us are here!" And that now appears in the catechism as a prohibition of suicide in general – clearly the only one that anybody could find in the whole Bible, fat as it is!'

The whole company was surprised. The old ladies said it was a silly catechism.

The girl in white, who had just been confirmed, said:

'Please, grandfather, give me the catechism.'

She took it and threw it through the open window of the balcony down on to the street with a movement of infinitely gentle pleasure.

'Ugh! It is starting to get cold in here after all,' said the hostess, and closed the balcony door.

'Well,' came the distinguished young opera singer's deep, sonorous voice, 'it is still an act of cowardice to take one's own life.'

The old ladies on the sofa leapt up with delight: 'Yes, what a cowardly thing it is to commit suicide!'

'Hmm,' said the bank manager Israel, 'hm, that's why we have to read at school the dreadful examples of that cowardly Lucretia, and the spineless weakling Hannibal, and that frightened old wretch Cato – in short, all those who were too cowardly to look life in the face and ignominiously ran away from history.'

'Yes,' it was the red lady who cut in, 'yes, not to mention Judas Iscariot, who went and hanged himself like a coward, though he could very well have bought himself a plot of land for his silver pence and atoned for his sin by leading a virtuous life...'

The distinguished opera singer had not expected these examples; he slipped out into another room, humming an aria from *Pajazzo*.

'Well,' said the old professor, 'it is true, of course, that it may not require any specially superhuman courage to take one's own life. It is possible to think of cases where it takes more courage to live though it may be tempting to die. But as far as we can judge with our own eyes, the courage which is needed to continue a miserable and meaningless life is infinitely more widespread than the courage which is necessary to commit suicide.'

The old gentleman was sitting with his eyes closed as he spoke, and he didn't notice that one after another the company was beginning to tire of this uncomfortable subject and move away across the room.

At last only the girl in white was left.

'Dear grandfather,' she said, 'you have such a lot of curious ideas. And it is a pity that some of them are right, and could make people's lives greater and freer and more worthwhile if only they would take them seriously. But when people sense you are serious they run away.'

THE SIXTH SENSE

(Det sjätte sinnet, 1900)

Once upon a time there was a princess...

We did not know she was coming until suddenly she was standing among us, beaming with life, glittering with diamonds and wearing an enormous Asiatic order on her generously proportioned bosom. A deathly hush fell upon the room. The hostess rushed towards her with outstretched arms, flushed with delight that she actually had come; for she was not just an ordinary princess. She was not the daughter of some king or emperor, but the daughter of Lundholm the tanner in Södermalm, and she was the widow ofa Kalmuckian diplomat who had held the legitimate title of aprince because he was related on his mother's side to the Khan ofBukhara and was descended through his paternal grandmother in direct line from the immortal Genghiz Khan. She was immeasurably rich. She had a desert in Turkestan with fishing rights in the Aral Sea, a castle in the Causasus, a hotel on the Avenue Ruysdaël and a house in Tjärhovsgatan.

After a while we settled down again. It was a small select gathering. Two or three important poets, a few important painters and composers and an important leading actor, together with some ministers of state and attachés.

I paced up and down the room and I sniffed now and then at a giant pale-blue agapanthus which the most beautiful of all the ladies had taken from her belt and given me as a token of secret understanding. But it no longer had any scent. And occasionally, as my thoughts wandered, I drank a glass of some alcoholic beverage. Our host, the affable Consul General, asked me what I šthought about Nordlund, the murderer. I replied that I could not approve of his conduct.

The princess was sitting upon a gilded table relating tit-bits of information about her visits to several of Europe's courts. The King of Denmark had joked with her. The Prince of Wales had served her a cup of tea. She also said something about Princess May of Teck. She talked about these things in a perfectly ordinary way, without any affectation, and she did not appear to regard them as unduly important. The ladies made a circle round her and listened with tears in their eyes.

'How natural and charming she is!' the girls whispered to each other. 'You would hardly believe she is a princess.'

I approached the lady who had so very kindly given me an agapanthus.

'Madam,' I whispered, 'I love you.'

'Yes,' she replied, 'isn't she absolutely delightful!'

In the smoking room sat the poets talking shop. One of the painters was improvising on the piano. The leading actor stood motionless in the middle of the floor, like a statue.

Suddenly the Princess leapt gracefully down from her table and switched off the electric light. Then she sat down on a cushion on the floor. The ladies let out a cry of delight and made a gypsy-camp all round her. She began to talk about ghosts and spirits and God in a light, chattery tone, as unaffected and natural as a moment before when she had been talking about the King of Denmark. The painter stopped improvising, the poets issued forth out of the smoking room like bears coming out of their lair, and our host, the Consul General, took me aside and whispered:

'You had better try to keep serious now.'

The lady who, with an air of incomparable pleasure, had loosened an agapanthus from her belt and given it to me was now sitting at the feet of the Princess and gazing into her eyes as she spoke of ghosts and spirits and God. And Mary of Bethany never wore so beatic an expression as she lay at the feet of the Master.

'Yes,' one of the poets said, 'the Princess is quite right: there are ghosts. Out in the country, where I live, we have a ghost that wears a black coat and a top hat. It often moves past me in the dark when I cross the hall. Its favourite place is by the telephone.'

A slight shudder went through the whole company. Once could feel it in the air.

'My housekeeper has seen it too, and so have the maids. My housekeeper says the ghost's name is Gavelius or Gavell or something like that. However, I would not consider if justified to argue from the existence of ghosts, which is indisputable, to the existence of God or the immortality of the soul.'

The Princess gave him an indulgent smile and reproached him amiably with a raised forefinger:

'Doubter!' she said. 'And you, who have the sixth sense! You do have it, you must not deny that. It is more finely developed in you than in most people, otherwise you would not be the poet that you are.'

The poet did not reply. He was also deep in thought.

'Excuse me, Princess,' I shyly broke in, 'I have admittedly never had the privilege of seeing a ghost on my own account, but my grandmother has seen any number of them. Nearly all old ladies see plenty of ghosts; it would therefore never occur to me to question their existence. But I have never heard my grandmother speak of the sixth sense. She became acquainted with her ghosts exclusively by means of the usual five senses: mostly by vision, quite often by hearing or feeling, not so often by taste and smell. I think I once read in an English novel about a ghost that consisted only of a nasty taste in the mouth. What would we be actually supposed to do with the sixth sense?'

'You have completely misunderstood me,' the Princess replied in a rather cold tone, shaking her head with impatience. 'The sixth sense is perhaps a misleading expression, I will concede you that – it is not to be understood as a "sense" of the same kind as the other five and on the same level – no, it is a spiritual gift of an infinitely higher nature. I would characterize it as an inborn leaning towards spirituality, a sense for the higher things in life, an ability to guide one's lower, outward senses so that one can see ghosts – it is a foolish habit you have of calling spirits "ghosts", do you call God a ghost? – so that one can see spirits and speak with them and understand them. The sixth sense is actually present in all of us. In the lower kind of people it is weak, but in higher natures it is lively and well-developed. A time will come when a person will be valued not for the number of ghosts – spirits, I mean – that he has seen, but for their quality.

'In the case of my friend,' the Princess continued, hardly pausing for breath, 'in the case of my friend the Baroness von Ehrensteiss* of Trapezunt the sixth sense is especially highly developed. Some time ago she had a conversation with my husband's spirit. He revealed himself to her in a dream. It was matter of the very highest importance that he had to communicate to her – I cannot tell you what it was, for it was absolutely private. However – yes, you think of course that it was just a dream, like all other dreams – but if you pay attention to one little detail that I will tell you then you will have to change your opinion. My husband – my husband had a birthmark – on one thigh, directly above the knee. Well, this birthmark – which Baroness von Ehrensteiss naturally could not possibly have ever been able to see in the flesh, she could never have had the slightest inkling of its existence – she saw this birthmark quite plainly in her dream!'

There was thoughtful silence. The ladies sat as if they were in church. The gentlemen stared solemnly at their finger-nails or at the clouds of smoke from their cigarettes. I sniffed at my agapanthus.

---

* Translator's note: Söderberg's original readers would recognize the German for 'Honourable Rump'.

THE CONSUL GENERAL AT THE PALACE BALL

(Generalkonsuln på slottsbal, 1904)

On the 21st of January this year, as in all previous years for as far back as he could or wished to remember, Consul General Rubin had been invited to the palace ball, and he had very nearly finished dressing for the occasion. He spent a long time turning out a drawer of his secretaire and found to his vexation that he did not have a really clean white cravat; but it no longer mattered so much, since it would anyway be as good as hidden under the green neck-band of the Vasa Order. For at last he had actually become a Commander of that Order. And he made no attempt to hide from himself the satisfaction which that gave him. He was now just fifty years old, and at that age a man *ought* to be a Commander. Each time of life has its particular pleasures; at the age of thirty or so a simple little star on one's dinner-jacket is most agreeable, though etiquette requires that one should joke about and give the impression that one acquired it as a result of some unfortunate accident. But at the rank of Commander life becomes serious; then joking stops, or else it has a hollow ring of envy about it which makes it as good as direct flattery. His other orders really only reminded him of past hopes which had not, or had only partially, been realized. "L'instruction publique" with its mauve ribbon reminded him that he had really desired the red ribbon of the Legion of Honour, and though his St Olav was mostly red he had, at the time when he received it, been entertaining foolish dreams of the Northern Star with its dignified black. But given the honourable ribbon of a Swedish Commander as a background, even these minor glories took on a new dignity. And this was still more the case with the big shimmering gold cross of the Order of the

Alligator, which was hanging on a splendid colourful ribbon across the dressing-table mirror. That was a token of recognition from the South American republic of Mondego, whose somewhat limited interests in Stockholm Rubin had for many years cared for, and not without delicacy, in his capacity as Consul General. His friend Don Manuel Garcia, the President, with dictatorial powers, of that charming little transatlantic republic, had sent him the attractive decoration some five years ago in remembrance of his discreet help in a case of financial embarrassment during some happy days they spent together at Monte Carlo. But he had not dared to wear it until now; for it looked altogether too outlandish, and there was furthermore a rather wide gulf between a big cross and the little trifles on his coat-lapel. That gulf had at last been bridged by the ribbon of a Commander of the Vasa Order, and so with an easy conscience he took up the Order of the Alligator from his mirror and hung it for the first time over his red, gold-braided dress coat. Now he was ready; and as he looked at himself in the mirror there was only one thing he would have wished to alter – himself. For he prided himself on being no fool and also on being a pretty good judge of people; and that is why he attached so much more importance to his decorations than to himself.

*

It was a fine evening, not too cool, and glittering with stars. Rubin decided to go on foot; for it was a reasonably short walk. The clock at St James's pointed to half past eight. That meant that he was much too early and could do as he pleased for a good hour. He hesitated by the door of a house, where an old friend of his lived. Should he go upstairs and sit talking for a while? But no, it wouldn't be right just now. His friend, whose position in life was more humble than his own, might easily get the idea that he was trying to impress him with his finery. He went on.

He stopped by the window of a little cigar-shop and smiled amiably at his own portrait, a crude but recognizable caricature that stared at him from the front page of a comic newspaper. The cartoon depicted a symbolic brawl between a number of leading figures in public finance, most of whom were more important and better known than he was, and in whose company he was pleased to see himself caricatured. In another such paper he saw another group of public figures, and these too were mostly his own friends and acquaintances.

'A little country and a little town,' he thought. 'We are such a tiny handful of figures who act on this stage, always the same people – and in a little while I shall meet the whole bunch of them at the palace. But to think that the Swedish people are interested in us and our little affairs is surely just an illusion in the heads of the people who edit comic newspapers. Still, I don't have anything against...'

'Good evening, mandarin! On your way to see the King, I should think, to judge by the rig-out!'

The voice of a woman. Rubin looked round.

'Klara! It has been such a long time! You are putting on weight.'

'Oh well, business is pretty good. I have just closed shop and I am on my way home. If I did not imagine you have other plans, I wonder if I might invite you home with me for a whisky?'

Rubin looked at her for a moment before he replied and in a single quick glance under the gaslight he assessed the marks which the past four or five years had made on her appearance. Klara Liebmann... So slim and slender she had been. In those days she had worked in a perfume shop. Now she had a business of her own, which he and a few other friends had helped her to set up. They had never had any illusions about their relationship, and they had parted amicably. He had never really got over the vague sense of miscalculation which her cheerful talk and her natural good humour made him feel – for his first impression of her had been of two intense black eyes in a pale face which had passed him in the dusk one windy autumn evening and which had led to expect and hope for something quite different. But that was in the past. Now her face showed absolutely no sign of anything other than a gay life and a rather rich diet.

'Well, well!' he replied, 'so you have whisky at home, do

you? Ah well, I don't suppose His Majesty will be expecting me just yet. I can spend half an hour with you.'

He looked at his watch.

'Do you still have your little flat?'

Yes, she still had it; it was only a few streets away.

*

Rubin walked up and down in the three little rooms, while Klara took out a decanter, two bottles of soda-water and two glasses from a little corner-cupboard in traditional folk style, with painted hearts and tulips. Rubin stopped and looked at it; it had been added since his time, together with a wall-tapestry and some cushions in the same style. 'It appears that Skansen* is expanding,' he said.

And then he added:

'My wife is very fond of that style, too.'

Otherwise, things in the flat had not changed very much. On all the side-boards and tables there were lots of framed photographs as before, though not entirely the same ones as before. He couldn't help looking for a portrait of himself and at last he found a tiny one in a corner over the tiled fireplace.

She mixed him a drink.

'Don't make it too strong,' he asked.

He sank back into a large leather-clad basket-chair which he once, long ago, had bought and given her so as to have at least *one* piece of furniture there that he liked – otherwise he had let her litter the place up according to her own taste.

'Don't you think we ought to have a fire as well?' she said.

'There is wood in the stove already, it only wants lighting.'

But the wood was damp and refused to burn. She went out to the kitchen to fetch the paraffin-can, tossed a sprinkling of paraffin over the wood in her old Bohemian way and lit the wood again. The fire flared up until the chimney whistled and

* Translator's note: Skansen is the name of the famous Folk Museum in Stockholm.

sang and the glare of the flames flashed brightly over the red hearth-rug.

'There!' she said. 'Now the labourer is entitled to her reward.'

And she made a drink for herself, sat down in the corner of the sofa, raised her glass to him and drank.

They talked a little about the ways of the world and about mutual friends, but at times there were some very long pauses.

'How odd,' Rubin thought to himself. 'Four years ago there were times when I almost believed I was in love with her, and now we have practically nothing to say to each other but *skål!*'

'What are you thinking about?' she asked.

He replied: 'Nothing at all. *Skål!*'

On the table beside him lay a pile of picture postcards – landscapes, folk costumes and variety stars all mixed together. He picked them up and looked at them absent-mindedly. One of them showed a Lapp girl with dark eyes, a smile that revealed her white teeth and a cheeky tuft of hair peeping out under her pointed bonnet. He looked up, surprised:

'But surely, it's *you*?' he said.

'Yes,' she replied. 'A couple of years ago somebody dressed me up and photographed me for a picture-postcard firm. I'll give you one if you like.'

'Please yourself,' he said.

He had let the unfriendly reply slip out without thinking. He was angry with himself, but now it was too late. There was sharp, vicious glint in her eyes. She snatched the card from him with a little jerk, stood up and started to walk up and down the room whistling to herself. He said nothing, but took a long sip of his whisky.

'It was a strong drink you made for me,' he said for the sake of saying something.

She stopped whistling and suddenly stood still behind his chair.

'Listen,' she said, 'there is something wrong with your collar. The gold braid has come loose. I will put it right for you with a little pin. Don't worry, I can do it so that the pin won't be visible at all. – Like this,' she fingered at his collar so gently that he could scarcely feel it, 'there – now it is all right. And now you can thank me. What on earth would the King have said if you had arrived at his palace with loose braiding on your collar?...'

And she pressed a little kiss upon his neck.

It gave him some pleasure to see that she was in a good humour again; he felt that he ought to kiss her, but she wriggled free and anyway his attempt was rather lame and led to nothing.

'Now you must go, my friend, or else you'll be late.'

She quickly helped him on with his fur coat, he emptied his drink, kissed her formally on the hand and left.

*

Sirius was shining right over the palace facade.

'She is a nice girl, Klara,' thought the Consul General as he walked across Norrbro Bridge, 'and I shall not forget her if she needs my help one day. But the drink was a little too strong.'

Under the palace arches a remnant of his old sense of reverence overcame him, and Charles XII's bodyguard on the stairs gave him a vague feeling that Sweden's history was still proceeding at full speed and that he himself had a part in it. But when, after shaking as lightly as possible the hand of the first palace marshal, he found himself in the company of old comrades and friends, he felt quite at home as usual and he only experienced – as usual – a slight unease because his uniform coat was red. He would rather have had it in the same dark blue as an ordinary Swedish civil uniform, but it couldn't be helped.

A little Russian attaché who had been home with him for dinner a few days ago gave him his hand with a little bow.

'Well,' asked Rubin, 'is it going to be war?'

'Like hell,' answered the Russian in French. 'We have no reason to look for a war with Japan just at present. Indeed, from several points of view it would be rather inconvenient. And the way things are *we* shall be the ones who determine the date for the outbreak of hostilities. If Mutsuhito or whatever his name is really does want a beating to remember us by then he will have to be so good as to wait a little.'

The Consul General had in his youth been to Southern China on a business trip and therefore regarded himself as something of an expert on Japan.

'I feel sorry for Mutsuhito,' he said. 'He is far too clever to wish for a war with Russia; but he could be driven to it by his people. That's how it is these days – the war-lust of the princes is a thing of the past. Now it is the people who...'

He went on undaunted, but, as sometimes happened when he spoke French, he fell into old phrases which were stored up in his brain and which led him away from what he really meant to say until he forgot it and said something else, sometimes the very opposite. As he was talking, his eyes wandered towards a mirror. It struck him that an empty space had developed at his back – it was almost as if people were forming a semicircle behind him – and he saw in the mirror two lieutenants with their hands over their mouths eyeing him in a peculiar way. What could it be that they found so funny? He could see nothing apart from the Russian whom he was talking to, and he did indeed look a little comic, but after all...

Suddenly he saw in the mirror the Chamberlain von Pestel – one of his wife's cousins – coming up to him and felt his hand touch him gently on the shoulder.

'Good evening, my old friend,' said Pestel. 'Where have *you* come from?'

'What do you mean?' asked Rubin.

Pestel had removed something from his collar – a little card, which he handed to Rubin. Rubin stared in bewilderment at the face of a pretty girl with smiling white teeth and with a tuft of black hair peeping out under a pointed Lapp bonnet.

'What is that?' he stammered.

'An unauthorized decoration,' said Pestel.

THE CHINESE

(Kinesen, 1905)

I woke up last night and could not get back to sleep again. It was not dark and not light in the room, for it was a summer night. Strips of milky light mixed with ash-pale shadows. There were little spots and points of light and narrow bright streaks in the mirror on the wall and in the three-sided brass arms of the chandelier. The window was open. I heard voices from the street and stifled laughter. Between the slats of the venetian blind, which was green in daylight but was now dark grey, there shone a red star. I decided it must be Mars. There are plenty of red stars, but the sky was not dark enough for any of the fixed stars to be shining so brightly, and of the planets the obvious one to think of was Mars.

I lay there going over old thoughts and memories, some of them sad, most of them completely meaningless. In my ears I kept hearing a tune that I detest. I thought to myself:

'It clearly is not our will that decides which melodies rise up in our soul, or whether we hear any melody at all. It is also not my will that decides which thoughts come to me, or whether I have any thoughts at all. And my will, is it controlled by myself, my conscious self? Far from it. I often wish things that I wish I did not wish – '

If only I could get to sleep.

The star kept on shining pale and red in the ash-grey sky. An old verse rose up in my memory:

> Men live their lives
> Always alone.
> Like stars they pass
> And do not meet.

Where did I get that from? Oh, I remember. It is a Chinese poem by Li Po, 'the immortal who loved to drink'. He drank rice sake from a china cup. Often he looked too deeply into the cup. And that was the death of him, for one night, when he had emptied many cups, he tripped on the gangplank of his patron's pleasure boat and drowned in the Yellow River. That was about the same time as Ansgar was preaching Christianity in this country, I suppose, and turning people's values upside down... Yes, how time flies!...

Have I ever met a Chinese? No... – Oh yes, I have. At one of the big hotels here in town one of the waiters at one time was Chinese. God knows how he got there. His job was to speak English, but he also spoke Danish. He was of slender build and had a face like a child's. His skin was pale brown, and he reminded me very much of Chulalongkorn and his Siamese who were here in '97. His eyes were attractive, gentle and intelligent. Round his lips he had a network of those fine old-age wrinkles and folds which are characteristic of the ancient races of the Far East.

It was in the days soon after the Battle of Mukden. I tried to lead him into temptation by asking 'Are you Japanese?' He answered in a low, soft voice with a slightly religious tone 'I come from China.' 'And where from then?' – 'Sang-hay' – 'Oh, Shang-hai...'

I watched him closely as he served a party near my table, some members of the First Chamber. He made a most civilized impression beside them. And I had to chuckle to myself as I watched their elephantine bodies, their lumpy, puffed-up faces and their waxy, colourless eyes and remembered how at school we were taught that the ideal of human beauty is represented by the Germanic race. And there was no possible doubt that this still was the opinion of these senators.

But the little Chinese was popular with the guests and an object of universal interest and he got generous tips; and when his fellow-waiters of Aryan descent noticed that, their faces became yellower than his and their eyes looked more squintily at him than his at them, and one of the more racist of them stood in a corner clenching his fists under the napkin and seemed to be practising boxing movements...

> Men live their lives
> Always alone...

I lay with my eyes closed so as to sleep, but a cool wind over my eyelids forced me to open them. A moth had flown into the room and went back and forward for a while in the ash-grey half-light and then was silent and gone. Through the window I heard a drunkard's staggering steps along the pavement. And the star glittered.

I looked and thought of the well-known telescopic picture of Mars with its wonderful network of dead-straight 'canals' or vegetation strips. And I knew that these straight lines proved that the planet must be inhabited. We know from spectrum analysis that it is made up of roughly the same elements as the earth. But in their natural outcrops, fissures and contours these elements never form a straight or anywhere near straight line of any considerable length. No river, no coastline, no mountain ridge and no natural belt of vegetation forms a straight line. The straight line is a product of art; it is a correction of the vagaries of nature. What sort of beings can they be who irrigate their fields with these absolutely straight canals? Do they perhaps know more about our planet than we do about theirs? Are they at this moment making poems to express the same melancholy feeling as the Chinese poet expressed a thousand years ago? Did they think ten thousand years ago the thoughts which are now called new and dangerous down here? It is clear that one species, one form of life must there, as here, have seized power over all the others in order to impress upon that little planet the mark of their will and their needs. But is that life-form anything like man? Or is it perhaps some kind of giant ant with strong social instincts and highly developed engineering skills but no aptitude for philosophy? Does their race live and work in this present time, or did they perhaps die out long ago, just leaving behind the dark network of water and greenery in the red desert sands as a sign of their brief existence?

Useless questions. If only I could get to sleep!

The second time I saw the little Chinese was one wild night in the big hotel's restaurant. There was a group of us from the world of books, pens and pads. Markel was with us, and he was drunk. He talked philosophy with the Chinese. It goes without saying that the sort of philosophy that an old Uppsala student – even if he had not been under the influence of strong drink – can talk with a Chinese waiter must be of the most general kind.

'Dear little Chinaman,' he said, 'what do you think about death?'

The face of the Chinese betrayed the fact that he was trying to conceal his surprise at being asked what was, in the circumstances, so strange a question. To talk of death with a stranger is in the highest degree improper. And this strange devil was visibly drunk and would have been even in a sober condition a boorish person. His face tried to hide these thoughts, and he clearly wanted to avoid having to answer the question. But Markel repeated it:

'Dear little Chinaman, I swear by all the devils and dragons in the world you will get no bloody tip from me if you don't tell me what you think about death.'

The Chinese smiled affably, pale under the brown skin. He thought carefully before answering. In his face there was a firm resolve not to say what he thought, but what might be most suitable. And therefore he finally gave the reply which Confucius once gave one of his disciples in answer to the same question, and which he – the waiter – had most probably had to learn as a small child in a primary school in Shanghai:

' – We do not yet know what life is; how, then, shall I be able to say anything concerning death?'

This reply came with a polite smile, in a Danish that was beginning to sound slightly Swedish. And he recited it with a fast tongue, like a response out of the catechism, which perhaps is what it really was.

We looked at each other in surprise. Markel became wild with delight. He wanted to embrace the Chinese. He practically hailed him as a brother. He said he would travel to the Far East and take him with him. He pulled some banknotes out of his trousers pocket and tried to force them upon him, but the Chinese retired, bowing and smiling, and the banknotes fell on the floor. We prepared to leave. In the foyer the Chinese came and gave the banknotes to one of us in a carefully wrapped package. Markel was already out on the street, where he was getting familiar with a coachman –

Outside I could hear the sound of brooms sweeping the street. Daylight was beginning to appear, and the red star was becoming more pale.

Again I tried to guess what sort of shape and form the rulers of the little red planet might have. Human beings like ourselves they cannot be, unless by some highly improbable coincidence of entirely identical circumstances. I tried to imagine them as extremely clever, intelligent elephants, perhaps furnished with wings. I thought of them as large birds with their claws evolved into very capable hands. But then I remembered that with birds everything has to be very light, including the brain, and that the lightness of the winged creatures in conquering gravity relieves them of one important reason for needing to exercise their intellect and inventiveness. No, earthbound, tied to the earth and longing to rise above it, driven along by the harsh demands of a thousand necessities, that is what those beings must be like which are to be able to break free from the limits of their own existence, to surpass themselves and transform their world to suit their own convenience...

If only I could get to sleep!

Just once more I saw the little Chinese. It was an early summer morning by the waterfront at the Strömparterre. I had gone out there now, while it was empty and quiet under the big trees, had got away from the hellish noise on the streets and squares to squeeze the juice out of a lemon and to read a book. There was nobody there except myself and the Chinese. He stood bending over the railings looking down into the fast-flowing current. I was sitting at a table not far from him. I didn't notice him until he turned to me and said good morning. I replied to his greeting. Now, without his uniform and exposed to the merciless sunshine,

I thought he looked poor and sick. He was standing so close to me that I thought I ought to say something.

'It is beautiful here, don't you think?' I asked.

He considered a little, as if he needed time to understand the question. Then he replied:

'It is strange.'

He passed me slowly, stopped a little further along and stood by the railing looking down into the water.

The next day I went into the restaurant.

'What has happened to the Chinese?' I asked the waiter who was pouring my coffee.

He was a well-fed young man who moved his elbows smoothly and had the head-waiter's baton in his knapsack.

'He has left,' he replied.

And he added in a half superior, half apologetic tone:

' – He didn't fit in here.'

*

The star has faded and gone away. A milk-cart is rattling along the street.

If only I could get to sleep!

THE BURNING TOWN

(*Den brinnande staden*, 1905)

Through the two windows of the room with their bright lattice-work blinds shines the clear winter sunlight in two long diagonal patterns across the soft green rug, and on the warm sunny patches a little boy is dancing up and down. He does not know very much about the world yet. He knows that he is little and he is going to grow up, but he does not know that he has been born or that he is going to die. He knows he is four years old and will soon be five, but he does not know the meaning of the word 'year': he still measures time only by 'yesterday', 'today' and 'tomorrow'.

'Daddy,' he suddenly says to his father, who has just finished breakfast and lit the first cigar of the day – for *he* measures time by cigars – 'I dreamed such a lot last night! I dreamed about all this room! I dreamed about the chairs and the green rug and the mirror and the clock and the big stove and its doors and its little shelves!'

And he runs up to the stove where the morning fire is blazing and crackling away and does a head-over-heels in front of it. He regards the stove and the place in front of it as the best and most important part of the room.

His father nods genially over the top of his newspaper. And the little boy laughs back at him wildly. He is at the age when laughter still expresses simple joy, and not a sense for the comical. The other evening he stood in the window and laughed at the moon, not because he thought the moon was funny but because he was delighted at the sight of its round shiny face.

When he has finished laughing he gets up on his knees on a chair and points at one of the pictures on the wall. 'And most of all I dreamed about that picture,' he says.

The picture is a photographic reproduction of an old Dutch master called *A Burning Town*.

'Well, what did you dream about it?' asks his father.

'I don't know.'

'Oh, try to remember!'

'Well, I dreamed that there was a fire and I patted a dog.'

'But you are afraid of dogs!'

'Oh yes, but on pictures I can pat a dog a little bit.'

And he laughs and dances up and down.

Then he comes back to his father and says: 'Take the picture down, daddy! I want you to show me the picture again as you did yesterday.'

The picture is a newcomer to the room. It only arrived the day before. The little boy has long since got to know the other pictures round the walls, Uncle Strindberg and Uncle Schopenhauer and Uncle Napoleon and ugly old Goethe and Granny when she was young. But the Burning Town is new, and apart from that it is a jollier picture than the others anyway. His father does as the little boy asks and takes the picture down from the wall and they look at it together. Over a broad river estuary which bends its way out to the sea and is full of boats and ships there is a bridge with rounded arches and a tower. On the left bank lies the burning town: rows of narrow houses with pointed gables and high roofs, churches and steeples; masses of people milling about in confusion, a sea of fire and flames, clouds of smoke, ladders propped against the walls, horses bolting away with their carts tipping over, the quay full of barrels and sacks and all sorts of lumber, on the river a crowd of people in a boat which is on the point of capsizing, people running for their lives across the bridge and right in the foreground two dogs stand sniffing at each other. Deep in the background, where the river broadens out towards the sea, a much too little moon sits upon the horizon in a haze of faint clouds and looks down on all the misery with a pale, sad face.

'Daddy,' the little boy asks, 'why is the town burning?'

'Somebody has been careless with fire,' says his father.

'*Who* has been careless?'

'Well, one can't exactly know that so long afterwards.'

'How long afterwards?'

'It is several hundred years since that town was burnt down,' says his father.

The little boy will not be any the wiser for that answer, his father knows very well, but he has to say something. The boy sits quietly for a moment meditating. New ideas and new conceptions of things are moving about in his brain and jostling with the old ones. He points with his tiny fingers touching the glass over the burning town and says:

'Yes, but it was burning yesterday, and it's burning today as well, isn't it?'

His father tries to explain the difference between pictures and reality. 'This is not a real town,' he says, 'it is only a picture. The real town was burnt down a long, long time ago. It's gone now. The people who are running about here and waving their arms are dead now and they don't exist any more. The houses have burnt down. The steeples have collapsed. The bridge has gone, too.'

'Did the steeples burn down or fall down?' asks the boy.

'They burned *and* they fell.'

'Are the steamers dead too?'

'The boats have been gone for a long time,' says the father. 'But they are not steamers, they are sailing boats. There weren't any steamers in those days.'

The little boy sticks out his bottom lip and looks displeased.

'But I can *see* that they are steamers', he says. 'Daddy, what is *this* steamer called?'

He certainly has a mind of his own, this boy. His father is tired of answering questions and says nothing. The boy points his finger at the old Dutch merchant-ships and talks to himself: this steamer is called Brage, and this one is Hillerjö, and this is the Princess Ingerborg.

'Daddy,' he says all at once, 'is the moon gone too?'

'No, the moon is still there. That is the only thing in the whole picture that still exists now. It is the same moon as you laughed at the other day in the playroom window.'

Again the little boy sits quietly and meditates. Then comes another question:

'Daddy, is it a *very* long time since that town burned down? Is it as long ago as when we went into the country on the Princess Ingerborg?'

'It is much, much longer ago than that,' answers his father. 'When that town burned down, neither you nor I nor mummy nor granny existed.'

The boy's face suddenly turns very serious. He looks really worried. He sits quietly for a long time meditating. But it seems that he can't make all his thoughts fit together.

'Daddy,' he asks at last, 'where was *I* when that town burned down? Was it when I was in Gränna with mummy?'

'No, my lad,' his father replies, 'when that town burned down you didn't exist yet at all.'

The boy protrudes his bottom lip again with a face that says: No, this I *can't* accept. And he repeats emphatically:

'But where *was* I then?'

His father replies: 'You didn't exist at all!'

The boy looks up at his father with big eyes. Suddenly the whole little face lights up, he tears himself away from his father and starts to dance up and down in the patch of sunlight on the green rug and he shouts at the top of his voice:

'Oh yes, of course I did! *I* existed anyway; of course I did!'

He thought his father was just pulling his leg. This was obviously too crazy to be true! The maids sometimes told him tall stories for a joke, and now he thinks that his father is doing the same.

And he dances up and down in the sun.

THE KISS

(Kyssen, 1903)

Once upon a time there was a young girl and a very young man. They were sitting on a rock on a spit of land sticking out into the sea and the waves lapped right up to their feet. They sat silently, each of them wrapped in thought, and they watched the sun go down.

He was thinking that he would very much like to kiss her. As he looked at her lips it seemed to him that this was precisely what they were meant for. He had, of course, seen prettier girls and actually he was in love with another, but he would surely never be able to kiss the other girl because she was an ideal, a star, and 'die Sterne, die begehrt man nicht'.

She was thinking that she would very much like him to kiss her so that she would have an opportunity to be really angry with him and show how deeply she despised him. She would stand up, draw her skirts tightly round her, give him a look charged with ice-cold disdain and strut off, erect and calm and with no unnecessary haste. But so that he should not guess what she was thinking she said in a low, soft voice:

'Do you think there is another life after this one?'

He thought it would be easier to kiss her if he said yes. But he could not quite remember what he might have said on the subject on other occasions and he was afraid of contradicting himself. And so he looked deep into her eyes and said:

'There are times when I believe there is.'

This answer pleased her exceedingly well and she thought: I

---

* Translator's note: 'One does not desire the stars.' (Goethe)

like his hair, anyway – and his forehead, too. But it is a pity his nose is so ugly and he has no position – just a student reading for his exams. Not the sort of boy she could aggravate her friends with.

He thought: Now surely I can kiss her. But he was dreadfully frightened all the same, for he had never kissed a girl of good family and he wondered whether it was dangerous. Her father was lying asleep in a hammock not far off and he was mayor of the town.

She thought: Perhaps it would be better still if I were to box him on the ears when he kisses me.

And then she thought again: Why doesn't he kiss me? Am I so ugly and repulsive?

And she bent forward over the water to look at her reflection, but her image was broken by the splashing waves.

Her train of thought continued: I wonder what it will feel like when he kisses me. Actually, she had only been kissed once, and that was by a lieutenant after a ball in the town hotel. But he smelt so badly of punch and cigars, and though she had been rather flattered at being kissed by him since he was, after all, a lieutenant, she still felt that that kiss didnt amount to very much. Furthermore, she hated him because he had not courted her afterwards or indeed paid any attention to her at all.

And as they sat thus, each of them wrapped in private šthoughts, the sun went down and it became dark.

And he thought: Since she is still sitting by my side, even though the sun has gone down and it has become dusk, it may well be that she would not very much object if I kissed her.

And gently he put his arm around her neck.

She had not reckoned with this at all. She had thought that he would quite simply kiss her and then she would give him a box on the ears and strut off like a princess. But now she didn't know what to do. She wanted to be angry with him, of course, but she also didn't want to lose the kiss. And so she sat absolutely still.

Then he kissed her.

It felt much stranger than she had thought; she felt herself going weak and pale and she had quite forgotten that she was to give him a box on the ears and that he was only a student reading for his exams.

But he thought of a passage in a book by a religious doctor on *The Sex Life of Woman* where it said: 'One must take care that the marital embrace does not become dominated by sensual lust.' And he thought this must be extremely hard, since even a kiss could do so much.

*

When the moon came up they were still sitting there kissing.

She whispered into his ear:

'I loved you from the first moment I saw you.'

And he replied:

'For me there has never been anyone in the world but you.'

ARCHIMEDES' POINT

(*Arkimedes punkt*, 1898)

At one time I knew a horrible little street-urchin.

He was the same age as I was and lived in the same street. But he was superior to me in everything, not only in experience and daring, but also in knowledge; for with the help of a piece of chalk or coal he could cover the walls and fences of the little street with words and symbols I did not understand. When I wanted to go out, if I was alone and unprotected, I always stuck my nose out through the gate first and looked down the street to make sure that the little urchin was nowhere near. For he was stronger than I was and he resented the fact that my clothes were better and cleaner than his own.

One day I was given a sledge by my father. It was covered with a piece of flowery felt, the runners had sharp steel blades which reflected the sunlight and it had a little bell at the front. When I went down to the gateway with this sledge for the first time and the scent of newly-fallen snow in my nose made me sneeze, I was at once overcome by such mad delight that I totally forgot my usual precautions and went rushing out through the gate without looking either to right or left of me, jumping about and dancing like a puppet and shouting wild war-cries.

Just outside my gate the road began to slope downhill. I quickly sat astride my sledge and let it slide downwards; but the slope was not very steep and so my progress was slow and I had to help from time to time with my feet. An icy wind came up the street which started to make my ears cold, and it even began to chill my joy. As the icy cold was creeping in under my clothes, so the thought crept into my soul that I was no longer as happy as I had been a moment before when I had been coming down to the gateway with my sledge.

And while I was thinking that thought I suddenly saw the little street-urchin standing in his gateway with his hands in his trouser pockets. He was filthy, his hair was scurfy, and he looked frightful, and when I saw him my heart was filled with fear and anxiety, for he really was a dreadful ruffian.

I had no chance of getting away. I sat quite still on my sledge not moving a muscle, like a rabbit fascinated by a boa constrictor, and just waited for the boy to come out of his gateway and beat me up.

But my guardian angel was vigilant. The little street-urchin did not come out from his gateway; he just stood there with his hands in his pockets, contemplating me with indifference rather than hostility, and said:

'Clout yourself on the backside, kid, and you'll go faster!'

Then he took a lump of coal from his pocket, wrote a four-letter word on the wall and went in through his gate.

I went on riding down the hill and thrashed about with my feet to get forward, for the slope was not very steep. And then it suddenly struck me that there might be something in what the little street-urchin had said. When I am sitting on my sledge and somebody gives me a push in the back the sledge goes forward a bit. So if I now thump myself in the back it must naturally have the same effect as if somebody else did it. It was perfectly simple; what a fool I had been not to think of it before! I carefully looked around to make sure the little street-urchin was nowhere about, for I didn't want him to see that I was following his advice. And then I started to thump myself in the back as hard as I could.

But the sledge didn't budge. I thumped myself in the back till I was hot and red in the face, and two ladies stopped and laughed at me, but the sledge did not move.

Then I got cross and upset and took my sledge by the cord and ran home with it, wishing I had an elder brother who could beat the little street-urchin out of my way.

At the dinner table I told my father of my adventure and asked him to explain to me why it is that one cannot go forward on a sledge by thumping oneself in the back. My father did not laugh at me and he didn't tell me I was stupid as most fathers would have done, but he tried to give me a reasoned explanation of the phenomenon; but in so doing he got himself tangled up in contradictions so that I finally decided that he did not understand much more about it than I did. I then gave up hope of ever finding the solution to this problem and I asked my father if he would not at least beat up the little street-urchin. But he said he didn't have the time.

*

Time flies, the years pass.

The little street-urchin grew up and became a great lout. Myself, I went to school and learned all sorts of things; but I never found a quite satisfactory explanation of how it is that one cannot drive oneself forward on a sledge by thumping oneself in the back. It still happens at times that I lie awake at night pondering over this problem. And if one day I have a son and he asks me about this point I have firmly made up my mind to laugh at him and tell him he is stupid.

RUGG

(*Rugg*, 1901)

It is Sunday morning, and as I step out on to the porch I see the front drive before me, the gravel freshly raked. The cockerel, perched up on one of the gateposts, stretches his red comb high up into the sky and crows solemnly, three times. Down below the hens strut about, clucking to all their little chickens and teaching them godliness, morality and a modest, unassuming manner. On the other gatepost the cat sits with his tail wrapped round him. His eyes with their knifeblade pupils follow the flight of the birds over the tops of the pine trees; but he does not allow them to disturb his peace of mind, for he has learnt not to desire the unattainable. He has drawn a circle round himself with his tail and he cares nothing for the vanity and noise of the world outside. Anyway, the noise doesn't amount to much now on a Sunday morning; the cock has stopped crowing, satisfied with the traditional three calls; only the cow-bells are still heard from the slope over the road, and the pigs as they practise their French down in the sty: neuf-neuf, oui-oui.

But right in the middle of the drive lies the grey, shaggy, utterly nondescript dog Rugg. When he hears me coming out on to the porch, he lifts up his head, pricks his ears and watches me with two sparkling brown eyes; and only after I have called him by name: – 'Rugg!' – and snapped my fingers a little as a sign that I would like to talk with him, does he get up, stretch himself with a long yawn and come towards me, amiably wafting his tail. But this waft of tail is neither ingratiating nor particularly enthusiastic; it is something more than a mere formality, but not exactly an outburst of emotion. It is calculated to fit his estimate of my importance and my position in the household. For I am not his master, but his master's friend and for that reason I am also a friend of his.

'Rugg,' I say to him, 'just what kind of dog are you really? Your master says you are a damned mongrel; but since I am a guest in this house I will be polite to you and call you a dream dog. Your long body and short legs reveal that you are related to next door's wicked old dachshund. That rough coat has been handed down from some terrier or other among your ancestors on your mother's side; but your deceased mother was not a terrier herself – I knew her quite well and I still remember her cheerful bark when in the old days she used to come to meet me down by the crossroads; she was more like a poodle. But you yourself, Rugg, what are you like? Would you fancy trying to pass yourself off as one of those Dandie-Dinmonts that Walter Scott made fashionable in his country in his day; you are in fact faintly reminiscent of them from a distance.'

'No,' replies Rugg, 'don't try to tickle my vanity. I am glad I don't have any pedigree, and I don't see what's so special about being tied up howling for a whole week at a time at dog shows. I can do my job just as well without any medals. I guard my master's house and property, and my bark is deeper and stronger than the yapping of the little village mongrels round here, and that keeps the tramps away. And last autumn I killed a fox.'

'Cock-a-doodle!' says the cockerel on the gate-post to confirm the point.

And that is perfectly true: Rugg killed a fox, even though he looks so small and unimportant; and he saved the cock. I remember the occasion; it happened last autumn and I witnessed his exploit myself. I was a guest in the house at that time, as I am now. We had heard the fox first the previous evening when we were sitting at the table talking, while the wind whistled at the windows and Rugg lay on his mat by the door sleeping with one eye open. All at once he became restless and started growling and yapping, and then suddenly he leapt up wildly, barked like one possessed and jumped up at the door to get out. He paused at intervals to listen, with his ears pricked and his coat bristling. We too listened to the strange sound which the wind was carrying with it from the woods. It was the fox, who was sitting at the edge of the forest complaining about the bad times, for he had noticed that the hens were secured for the night. He sounded like a dog that was trying to bark but couldn't do it properly because he had a bad cold.

'Don't let him get out,' the lady of the house said, 'the fox will have him!'

'No,' said my friend, our host, 'Rugg is not big enough to fight the fox.'

Rugg had to stay indoors. It didn't help even when, with the foxiest of looks in his brown eyes, he lifted one leg against the wall in the hope of being chased out. That was an old worn-out trick and it was seen through at once. He got a smack from his master, crept under the table and forgot about needing to go out.

But the next day he took his revenge. We were playing croquet on the lawn in perfect peace when suddenly there was a dreadful hullabaloo in the back yard. Rugg was barking and the hens were cackling as if the Day of Judgment had come. 'The fox!' we all cried at once and rushed to the theatre of war with our croquet mallets raised up ready to strike. Naturally, the fox had made himself invisible at once; the hens were counted and found to be complete, and the cock had flown up on to a chestnut tree. He stayed up there for best part of an hour. Terror had suddenly taught him how to fly, but once he was safe he had forgotten that difficult art. Long after peace had been restored he remained sitting up there, measuring with his eyes the fearful distance down to the ground and cackling in embarrassment. In the end he had to be got down with a ladder. And only then did we see that he had lost a couple of his finest tail feathers. But where was Rugg? Rugg was gone. There was no point in whistling and calling; he had run off into the woods after the fox.

The lady of the house was disconsolate.

'Now the fox will get my little Rugg,' she said. 'I shall never see him again!'

For her the fox was a terrible wild beast.

I did my best to console her.

'Never give up hope that right will triumph,' I said to her. 'I know that Rugg is smaller than the fox; but he has more courage, and the feeling that he is carrying out his proper duty will make him strong. The fox on the other hand has a bad conscience, like Solness the builder in Ibsen's play.'

'That dog will look after himself,' said Rugg's master. 'His father's a dachshund!'

As we left the table after lunch Rugg came home from the woods. He had his tail in the air, his eyes were alight, and in his teeth he was carrying the fox's tail.

We stared in astonishment at each other and at Rugg. Had he really killed the fox, or had the fox given up his tail to save his life?

Rugg gave us a clear answer. Still with the tail in his teeth – it was no good trying to coax him to give it up – he set off towards the wood, but then stopped, put down the tail for a moment and barked sharp and clear.

'Come along!' he said.

We followed him and he showed us the way. Deep in the wood we found the fox, dead, bitten in the throat and the belly.

'That is a dachshund's bite,' said Rugg's master. 'But he must be a young fox. An older one would never have let himself be killed like that.'

He was a very young and very beautiful fox, red and white as a young fox should be. His legs and paws still had something of the pup's cheerful clumsiness. There was something innocent about him as he lay there: he had not had a long life, a long career of sinful adventures that might have left some dirty grey streak in his coat. We resolved to forgive him his criminal desire for the cock and to send his coat to the furrier to have a mat made out of it.

*

'Yes, Rugg,' I say to the dog when we have gone through this episode together in our memory, 'that was your great day, Rugg, and you are a remarkable dog.'

And it is true, the more I think of Rugg and his like, the more

I have to admire them. But when I examine properly my feeling for dogs and get to the bottom of it, I soon find that what I really admire most in them is my own nature, human nature. All our domestic animals, the cock up there on his gatepost and the cat on his, the cow in the paddock and the pig in the sty, all of them are to some extent our own work, the work of man. We have changed them all a little, toned down one quality and sharpened another; we have modified them to suit our requirements. But out of the wolf and the jackal we created something quite new when we made them into dogs, something whose like scarcely existed in all creation before us. No, in the case of the dog we were not satisfied with modifications; we changed him altogether, we made him the very opposite of what he had been before, taught him to hate his own flesh and blood and ally himself to man, his mortal enemy. In this world, where everything was hostile to us from the start, only the dog has learnt to see things from our point of view and to measure by our standards, to regard as good that which suits us and treat as evil that which is our enemy. The other animals which we have brought under our control serve us without knowing or wanting to. The cat catches rats entirely for his own pleasure, and he has never understood why those strange human beings praise him for catching a rat but beat him when he comes along with a heart full of innocence and a little bird in his teeth. He has given up pondering over the problem and does as he pleases anyway. The hen doesn't lay her eggs so that we can have French omelettes, the sheep doesn't offer us his wool as a tribute that he owes us, the cow may moo because she wants to be milked, but that is only because the pressure makes her uncomfortable. Only the dog has made it his pleasure and his highest endeavour to serve us willingly and knowingly.

Dogs have a religion and their god is mankind. And of all the world's worshippers the dog is probably the most decidedly monotheistic. He must have one master. I remember hearing about a guard dog who didn't know his master, because his master didn't bother about him. He was a hunter, the master; he kept beagles and greyhounds and despised the little black lump of a dog that guarded his house. But this dog chose himself instead a master of his own; he chose an old labourer, the oldest of them all, the one who had been longest on the estate. He attached himself to him, he obeyed no-one but him and followed him about whenever he was not tied up.

But precisely because man has created the dog in his own image I should find it just as difficult to say in general that I like dogs as to say that I do not like them. There is a sect among the Muslims of al-Kahira who regard as unclean those of their number upon whom in the course of the day the shadow of a dog has fallen. On Mäster Samuelsgatan in Stockholm there lives a middle-aged spinster who says her prayers every night together with her Moppe and shares not only her bed with him but also her toothbrush; and her heart would open itself in the same way for every Moppe in the world if only she could afford to pay for all the dog licences. The love of the Chinaman for his dogs steers a healthy middle course between these two extremes: he eats them.

And I for my part also steer a middle way, though rather differently ; I like dogs in much the same way as I like people, that is, with discrimination. Among dogs, as among people, there are geniuses and idiots, enthusiasts and philistines, philanthropists and born criminals. Among the dogs I have known personally I have met both clowns and serious folk, and I also recall one or two hypocrites who put on the mask of tragedy to hide a shallow soul. And dogs are like people also in another respect, namely that it is only possible to like them as individuals. Collectively they are almost always repulsive – just like people. If I am out walking along a pleasant path thinking about the ways of the world and I hear in the distance the noise of a rich landowner's dogs, I prefer to turn round and take another path. And I cannot deny that my love for animals cools down each time I see the vulgar rabble of big town dogs wildly pursuing a little bitch in full gallop across parks and plants, lawns and flower-beds.

However, the dog, as we now know him, is our own work, and there is hardly any vice or sin we could fairly blame him for in which we did not precede him and set an example. Also it is only by living together continuously with man that the canine race keeps going; we can safely prophesy that he will not survive us very long when the day comes for the fires to die out in our hearths and for our homes to fall into ruin. The little breeds will disappear, the big ones will forget what we taught them and become again what they were long ago, before they met us. And when no human voice any longer calls a dog, the dog also will have forgotten his language, and his old cheerful bark will be indistinguishable from the hungry howl of the wolf and the idiotic screech of the jackal.

The old story of the dog who laid himself down to die on his master's grave is a very clear symbol of the whole race's relationship to us humans, who have acquired from among our brother animals so many servants, but only one friend.

THE TALENTED DRAGON

(*Den talangfulla draken* 1913)

Once upon a time Pampus XIII was King of Pelargonia. He was from the beginning a pious, god-fearing king and a lover of peace, since he was not much good at war. But at last he became a mighty war hero, and that is what this story is about.

His queen, Pomponia, was fair and virtuous and very godfearing, and they had an only daughter, a lovely, delightful, shining pearl, the Princess Finissa, who was due to be married soon to her cousin, the Duke of Callipasta.

Word of this forthcoming marriage spread through the town until it came to the ears of Hannes Elsaffan, the young singer of songs; and thereupon he fell into a black despair. For he had seen the Princess Finissa one day when he had been summoned to the palace to sing his songs, and since that day he had loved her with a love that exceeded all reason and he likened her in his thoughts to a smiling moonbeam. But the Duke of Callipasta, who was a fat, flabby, arrogant prince, he likened in his heart to a great white louse. And Elsaffan, who dwelt with his old mother in a miserable shack on the outskirts of the town, went home and threw himself upon the old woman's breast and told her of his mad, hopeless love for the Princess Finissa. And when he would not leave off his weeping she tried to console him by telling him the story of *The Hungry But Ambitious Cat*:

An old, old woman, more wizened that a dead briar bush, lived in a little hut more fragile than a spider's web, more narrow than the closed fist of a miser and more dim than the understanding of a war-lord. She had a cat that had never set eyes upon anything that so much as resembled food but contented himself with sniffing at the scent of the mice in their holes and looking hungrily at the traces left by their feet. And if, on some rare occasion, he actually caught a mouse, he acted like a poor beggar who has found a great treasure: his face lit up and he said to himself: 'Ye gods! Is this a dream?' But one day, when he was almost dying of hunger, he jumped up on to the roof of the hut, and he saw on the neighbour's garden wall another cat, so fat that he could scarcely walk, strutting about like a lion with a measured and dignified air. At the sight of this the hungry cat let out a cry of astonishment and said: 'Sir, you look as if you have been at a banquet with the Emperor of China!'

'As a matter of fact, I *have* just come from the royal table,' said the fat cat; 'at dinner time each day I betake myself to the King's gate and I always find some fat piece of meat. That is my way of life.'

'Tell me, sir, I pray you,' said the poor cat, 'what do you mean by "a fat piece of meat"?'

The fat cat laughed, surprised at such ignorance:

'You common little wretch, fancy not knowing that! But you look the type. Your appearance is a disgrace to the whole feline race. You have eyes and ears and whiskers like a cat, but the rest of you looks more like a spider's web.'

'My noble brother,' said the poor cat humbly, 'you know that of all the animals we cats are the ones who most religiously observe the commandment to love our neighbours. Would you not therefore be so kind, sir, as to take me with you tomorrow when you go to the royal palace?'

'I suppose I could do that,' said the fat cat, 'for you look so shrivelled up that I cannot help feeling sorry for you.'

The thin cat returned home to the good old woman and told her of the new way of life that was opening up before him. But the old woman advised him to put aside such thoughts of vainglory and she warned him of the dangers that attend ambition. 'Those who are ambitious,' she said, 'are satisfied in the end only by the earth that rests upon their graves. Contentment is the only true happiness. Those who go out to seek their fortune must be taught that the gods only love him who is contented with his lot.'

But the hungry cat dreamed all night of the fat pieces of meat from the royal table and the next day he betook himself to the royal palace together with the fat cat. But before they had reached the palace he fell into one of the snares of Fate. Some archers had been sent out to kill certain cats that had been stealing fish and meat from the royal kitchen, and in order to trap the cats they had placed a big plate full of fat pieces of meat by the roadside. The hungry cat, having no sin upon his conscience, threw himself upon the meal with transports of delight; but he had hardly started eating when he was struck by an arrow. 'Alas,' he said as he took to flight, his poor blood running out from the wound, 'if ever I escape from this alive I will never again leave my little corner and my little mice.'

This sad story, which Hannes Elsaffan had heard his mother tell so many times of an autumn evening when he was a boy, gave him no consolation. He wept for three days and would not eat. But on the fourth day he went out into the wilderness to seek out an old prophet who lived as a hermit and was thought to have magic powers.

'Is it true that you can work magic?' he asked.

'It is both true and untrue. For I cannot do anything which is by nature impossible for a human being. But I have thought out a few things which other men will not discover for a few hundred or perhaps a few thousand years yet.'

'How do you mean?' Elsaffan asked in surprise. 'Will people in the future come to discover things which we and our fathers have not known? I was taught as a child that the wise ancients were the wisest of all men and that since their time mankind has become ever more foolish.'

'There is wisdom and wisdom. The wise men of old will always remain the wisest of all. But there will come a time when any fool can do a number of things which the wise men of old considered impossible. Tricks and trifles of no special importance. But what is it you want of me?'

'I do not even know that myself. But I am in love with the

Princess Finissa. Could you not arrange things so that I could see her sometimes?'

'Hm,' said the old man, 'it's Princess Finissa, is it? She is a lovely girl. I should fall in love with her myself if I were your age. But she is still nothing compared with the dancer Ylitta whom I knew in my youth. You should have seen her – ah!'

'But she is now dead and buried, and I am in love with the Princess Finissa!'

'Let me think,' said the old man. 'The princess is betrothed to the Duke of Callipasta. He is a stingy, sanctimonious, arrogant scoundrel and a year ago he cheated me of the fee for a little service I had performed for him. I would enjoy playing a trick on him. Hm! Princess Finissa lives in a tower of gilded copper and her balcony faces the sunset. Hm! I shall have to think about this. You had better come back in a week's time.'

'Will it cost very much?' Hannes asked with some embarrassment. 'I am afraid I have to tell you that I do not have very much money...'

'Nonsense!' the old man replied. 'A poor young man who is a poet and in love as well – I can help him for nothing.'

During the following week Hannes Elsaffan wrote the finest love-poems that were ever produced in the history of Pelargonian literature, and he set them to music and sang them in the evenings in the market place and he was given many a silver coin by the people. For he was known to all and he was well liked for his merry humour. And he not only sang his own songs, but he also told stories that he had learnt from his mother. And one evening, outside the Blue Lantern, he told this story of *The White Louse And Firejaws The Flea*:

The King of Lappatraskia, our traditional enemy, once had a large, splendid bed which was heaven itself, and in that bed dwelt a white louse which had grown big and fat by sucking the King's blood. One day, the far-travelled itinerant flea Firejaws came to pay a visit, but he was not made welcome according to the sacred laws of hospitality.

'My friend,' said the white louse, 'what are you doing here and where have you come from? This is, to put it plainly, no place for you. I suggest that you take your leave, for that would be in your own best interest.'

'But Your Excellency,' said the flea, 'what sort of a reception is this that you give me? I am not accustomed to such treatment. It is customary to say "How are you? Do sit down! I am delighted to see you!"'

'If you imagine,' the louse replied in a superior tone, 'that I am flattered at being called "Excellency", then you are quite mistaken. For I can tell you there is royal blood in my veins.'

'As far as that goes,' answered the flea, 'I am prepared to bet that before very long the same blood will flow in *my* veins. That is what I have come here for. I have been about in the world and I have tasted the blood of many different kinds of people. I like the blood of young girls most of all. But I have also dined with philosophers; their blood had a sour, bitter taste. The blood of poets I have also tasted; it was not very nutritious. I have just come now from a rich usurer; but he was a miser who made do with still worse food than the poets, and so his blood was the poorest fare I have ever had. But I have heard that the King eats a good deal of confectionery and drinks great quantities of wine, and so his blood ought to be sweet and tasty.'

'Quiet!' said the white louse, 'I can hear the King coming! You must keep still at least until he is asleep.'

And the King came in, heavy with wine, and cast himself upon his bed. But Firejaws was on him at once, biting him now here, now there, in a dozen places almost at the same time.

'Aaow!' said the King, 'what the devil is this? Vermin in the bed – in *my* bed? Servants ho! And bring torches!'

A few lord chamberlains in waiting rushed in with lighted torches and the King took a torch himself to investigate with. But he chanced to set fire to the bedclothes. In a moment the whole bed was ablaze, and the white louse, who on account of over-indulgence was slow in his movements, was burnt up together with the bed.

But Firejaws the flea had already hopped out of the window and journeyed on without a care in the world.

And the people listened to Elsaffan's stories, and his pockets jingled with little silver coins, and the landlord of the Blue Lantern charged nothing for the wine he drank, since he attracted many people to the place. And on the evening when he told the story of the white louse the Duke of Callipasta himself was among the audience. And His Grace laughed so much that he almost choked on his wine.

And Elsaffan resolved that evening to try to find some more stories about fleas and lice; for he had noticed that stories of that kind always went down well with the people.

But when a week had passed, he went out to the old prophet in the wilderness.

'Well,' he asked, 'have you conjured up anything for me now?'

'Mm – yes,' answered the old man, 'that depends upon you. Are you courageous and quick-witted? Can you play a part from start to finish without doing anything out of character?'

'I will try,' said Hannes Elsaffan. 'For the sake of the Princess Finissa I would try absolutely anything. But what sort of a part is it I am supposed to play?'

'You must realize yourself,' the prophet answered, 'that a poor poet cannot have any chance with the Princess. For her you must appear as something exalted, something far more exalted than the Duke of Callipasta. You must appear as the War-God Boomboom!'

'Saints preserve us!' said Hannes, 'how on earth could that be? Every little schoolboy knows from the catechism that the War-God Boomboom rides on a fire-spitting dragon. Where do I get one of those from?'

'I have conjured it up for you. Take a look at this!'

The prophet uncovered and showed Hannes a big dragon with shining metal scales of emerald green.

'Sit up on the dragon,' said the old man.

Hannes obeyed.

'Now turn that screw a little.'

He pointed to a screw in the dragon's neck.

Hannes turned the screw, and the dragon slowly and

125

majestically unfolded two large black wings.

'Now press that button just beside it. But hold tight! Keep firm hold of the steering – you steer him by his tail, and that is the control stick.'

The dragon rose up, slowly at first, then faster and higher, and flew about in great circles and flourishes wherever Hannes steered it. And the sun shone out through a cloud, and the cloud gradually came nearer and seemed to dissolve into mist.

'This way,' thought Hannes, 'I could go right on up to heaven, but I don't feel like it just at the moment.'

So he let the dragon down again and dismounted.

'Thank you very much,' he said, 'but why doesn't he spit fire?'

'He can learn to do that if need arises,' answered the prophet. 'But it would be foolish to let fly with fireworks when you are paying a nocturnal visit to the Princess. That would not be appropriate to the situation.'

'Do you not think,' Hannes reflected, 'that the War-God might be angry with me?'

'I should scarcely think so. He is an old Don Juan himself, and I expect he would just laugh over the story if he ever got to hear of it. Anyway, I believe he is a long way away; he has never made his presence felt in my lifetime, nor in my father's or grand-father's.'

'Some people say, down in the town, that you do not believe in the gods.'

'Quite right, my boy; I do not believe in them. But I worship them and sacrifice to them, and that is enough. Everyone should do that; it is, at any rate, the safest way. For if the gods do not exist, then they can do us no harm; but if, contrary to all probability, they do exist and I offer them no sacrifices, then they will be steaming angry with me, and no man should lay himself open to that risk! That was taught already in my grandfather's time by the wise prophet Pafnutius, who is known by the honorary title 'the Pascal of Pelargonia'.*

---

* Translator's note: The reference is to Pascal's notorious 'Wager': we should try

'How very curious!' said Hannes; 'but do you not think I ought to take a present with me for the Princess Finissa?'

'I have already thought of that, my lad. But it must be something unusual. Diamonds and long-tailed monkeys and openwork silk stockings and all such trash she has been thoroughly spoilt with; they would mean nothing to her. No, but now have a look at what I have devised.'

The prophet opened an old cupboard and took out something that looked like a bottle with a funnel to it.

'You see,' he said, 'I have discovered a method of storing human voices in bottles, so to speak. You stand here in front of the funnel and sing one of your best songs. Then you only have to turn this tap and the bottle will sing the song with precisely the same voice and expression as you! And it can sing that song as often as you like – in time the voice may come to sound a little cracked, but then everything in this world is subject to change...'

Hannes stood in front of the funnel and sang:

> It breaks the heart
> When lovers part;
> Do not forget me,
> Never forget me,
> Leonora!

'Leonora' was the name under which he had sung the praises of Princess Finissa. And, as poets do, he had sung of both the ecstasy of love and the bitterness of parting before ever he had experienced them. Poets always have been accustomed to draw on these experiences in advance, and on others too...

'Very good,' said the prophet. 'You really do sing beautifully and with feeling. You must give this bottle to the Princess so that she can hear your voice from it on the days

---

to believe in God, since we lose nothing if we are wrong but gain Paradise if we are right, whereas the atheist is a certain loser in either case. Söderberg paraphrased Pascal's argument in a posthumous note: 'It is all nonsense, but one has to believe it in order to be saved. Therefore I believe.'

when you are not with her. Then she will be quite certain that you are a god.'

'Thank you very much!' said Hannes Elsaffan.

The next evening, an hour after sunset, when the stars had begun to shine in the Pelargonian sky, he rode on his dragon to the Princess's copper tower. And he flew through the air, alone with the stars, while human beings were sleeping down below in the town, and he felt as though he were a god.

He stopped his dragon outside the Princess's balcony and knocked gently on the window. The Princess appeared inside with a pale, frightened face.

'Open, Finissa,' said Hannes Elsaffan. 'For I am the War-God Boomboom!'

Princess Finissa had, like all princesses, received a deeply religious education and her devotion to the War-God was especially warm; at the time of her confirmation she had even been secretly in love with him. She therefore did not hesitate for a moment to open up when she saw the War-God Himself riding on his dragon.

Hannes tied up the dragon to the balcony and went in to the Princess, who fell upon her knees and worshipped him.

'Rise up, my daughter,' said Hannes. 'I am indeed the God of War, yet I love you and my love transforms me almost into a mortal man when I am with you. Furthermore, I cannot reveal myself to human beings without borrowing the form of a real, living man. At first I thought of visiting you in the form of Prince Callipasta; that would have been most proper, as your father has chosen him for your husband. But I found him altogether too much like a lumbering great fat clodhopper. And so I took instead a handsome young man of the people with a good figure; I blew out his soul and shut it up in this bottle, and then I dressed myself in his form.'

'Lord,' said Princess Finissa, 'I have loved you and worshipped you for as long as I can remember. Is it really possible that you would have me for your wife?'

'Certainly,' said Hannes Elsaffan. 'We shall wed after the manner of the gods.'

And they did so.

But when dawn was approaching, the Princess said:

'Lord, what is the name of the man in whose form you have come to me, and what is his calling?'

'He is a singer of songs,' said Hannes. 'I know not what he is called, but I heard him singing in the market place when I had gone down into the crowd, invisibly, in order to make my choice. But he is an excellent artist and he deserves more encouragement from the court and the nobility than he has had so far. He sings with all his soul – indeed, his soul can sing even though it is parted from his body. Would you like to hear?'

He took out the bottle and made it sing *It Breaks The Heart*.

The Princess was moved to tears.

'Lord,' she said, 'I have a prayer to ask of you – please grant it! If you go down to the earth now at dawn and give back to the singer of songs his body and soul – who knows, some misfortune could always befall him, he might be killed or disabled, and on your next visit you would have to dress yourself in the form of some other man. And that would be a grief to me, I don't really know why... Besides, it is only too likely that the singer of songs has some girl whom he loves after the manner of common folk, and I cannot bear to think of that. Oh Lord, let me keep the bottle with his soul.'

'My beloved,' replied Hannes, 'how could I refuse a prayer from you?' And before he mounted his dragon and left her, he bade her promise most solemnly to keep their secret:

'All that touches the gods,' he said, 'must be veiled in secrecy. Our marriage therefore, must remain secret. You must not say anything about it, even to your parents.'

She promised this with a sacred vow. And in the morning at breakfast she took her mother aside and confided in her, under a promise of absolute secrecy, that the War-God Boomboom had visited her during the night, riding upon his dragon, and had taken her to wife after the manner of the gods. The pious Queen Pomponia hastened at once to King Pampus, who was still occupied with his morning toilet, and told him the news.

'Hm!' said the King. 'Hm! This sounds very mysterious. But this kind of thing has been heard of before. And if it is really true that I have acquired the War-God as a son-in-law – then, brother Hampus of Lappatraskia, we shall come and speak to you in plain Pelargonian!'*

The next evening after dark King Pampus and Queen Pomponia, together with the Prime Minister, the Minister for Foreign Affairs, the High Priest and the Editor of the state newspaper, all hid themselves on the roof of the copper tower. And when all of them with their own eyes saw the War-God come flying on his dragon, and the High Priest had distinctly recognized his face, all doubt was dispelled. King Pampus held a state council in the middle of the night and in the morning orders for mobilization were issued and war was declared on the King of Lappatraskia.

Unfortunately, the War-God Boomboom had not been invited to attend the state council; nobody dared to disturb him in order to ask his opinion on the matter. Consequently, the war correspondents who followed the early stages of the campaign did not exactly have the impression that the War-God was on the Pelargonian side. King Pampus was defeated in three battles and he was forced, with the remnants of his army, to seek refuge behind the walls of his capital. There was a long siege. The garrison was decimated and supplies began to run out. And one night Princess Finissa said to Hannes Elsaffan:

'I no longer know what to believe. Are you really the War-God? Why do you not help us against the King of Lappatraskia? Surely it would be quite easy for you – and by the way, I have never seen your dragon spit fire. Why doesn't he do that?'

'He is too clever,' replied Hannes. 'A fireworks display in the middle of the night would attract attention, and that is not the idea.'

---

* Translator's note: the Swedish Prime Minister Gustav Åkerhielm was dismissed in 1891 after a speech in which he had declared jingoistically that the time had come to 'speak to the Norwegians in plain Swedish'.

But the next day Hannes went to the old man in the wilderness.

'What shall I do?' he said. 'I am a man and I have been pretending to be a god. I did not believe for a moment that the girl would keep the secret, but I really couldn't have guessed that it would lead to a war! What on earth am I to do?'

'It is quite simple,' answered the prophet. 'You have taken on a part and you have to play it to the end. And, what is more, I will help you. Do you have the dragon with you?'

'Yes, here he is, the unlucky beast!'

'Good. Now it is time for him to learn how to spit fire!'

The old man took a bundle of rockets and stuffed them down the dragon's throat.

'When you press that button,' he said, 'he will spit fire. But that is not enough; he must also be able to sing the national anthem. It was originally, as you may know, a hymn to the War-God.'

And the old man took a bottle like the one Hannes had given to Princess Finissa but much bigger, and he placed it into a hole in the dragon's belly.

'I have certain knowledge,' said the prophet, 'that the King of Lappatraskia is planning to storm the city tonight after dark. You must then mount the dragon, be the War-God and put him to flight. When you press this button the dragon will spit fire and when you pull this lever he will sing the national anthem. It will be a brilliant success.'

That evening Hannes Elsaffan sat at home with his old mother, and she told him stories, just as when he had been a child. She told him the story of *The Purple Jackal*:

A jackal was being hunted by dogs and took refuge in a dyer's yard, where he jumped into a big vat filled with purple paint. When he came out again the dogs no longer recognized him but slunk away with their tails between their legs, as they were frightened by his bright colour. And when he returned to the woods the other animals did not recognize him either and could not believe that he was just an ordinary jackal. His bright colour filled them with fear and respect, and so they made him their king and gave him fine banquets. He appointed the elephant to be his prime minister, the lion his commander-in-chief, and the ass his archbishop. But one evening at dusk, when he heard the howl of his brother jackals some way off, he could not resist joining in their cry. Then the other animals realized that he was just an ordinary jackal and so they fell upon him and tore him to pieces.

'That served the stupid jackal right!' said Hannes.

At that moment he heard the Lappatraskians sounding their war trumpets in the dusk. He rushed out and mounted his trusty dragon. With great thrusts of his wings he hurried to the spot where battle had already commenced and the enemy were charging ahead singing their battle-song *Allons, enfants de Lappatraskia!* And Hannes made the dragon spit fire in all the colours of the rainbow, and then he pulled the lever and the dragon sang, with a voice like a hundred bassoons, the Pelargonian national anthem, *Ritsch, Ratsch, Filiboomboom-boom, Filiboomboomboom, Boomboom!* And now that the Lappatraskians saw the War-God Himself coming against them, spreading fire and destruction, they panicked and fled pell-mell, and the Pelargonians pursued them and cut them down in great numbers, and King Pampus himself mounted his white horse and with his own hands made cutlets out of the King of Lappatraskia, though he was his blood cousin. And when the battle was won Hannes Elsaffan continued for a while to fly in great circles over the city, and the dragon spat out its last rockets and sang the national anthem and all the people rejoiced and wept with emotion.

'This is the right moment for me,' thought Hannes Elsaffan.

'Now or never! I can't go on playing the War-God Boomboom for ever. Now I will descend with my dragon into the palace courtyard and I will go straight up to the King and ask for Finissa's hand. After my exploit today he can't refuse me, that is unthinkable. For I have saved the capital city and all the kingdom.'

As he approached the courtyard he saw the King, the ministers and all the court come rushing out of the palace in surprise and confusion. And when he landed with the dragon and set foot upon the ground they all threw themselves to the ground in silent, awe-struck adoration.

At the sight of this Hannes Elsaffan broke into a fit of wild, uncontrollable laughter.

The effect of this laughter was as sudden as it was unexpected. Everyone got up at once and stared at the War-God with astonishment and disapproval. For it was an article of faith in the age-old religion of the Pelargonians, handed down by their fathers and forefathers, that the gods never laughed, and no-one could imagine that even the War-God Himself would allow himself to laugh at the King. 'What sort of a specimen do you think you are?' said the King.

'Your Majesty,' replied Hannes, 'it is true that I am not the War-God but only the poor singer of songs Hannes Elsaffan. But I have put the enemy to flight, saved the capital city and all the kingdom, and I ask no reward but the hand of the Princess Finissa.'

The King went purple and stood there quite speechless for the whole of a minute.

'I have never heard anything so impudent in all my life,' he said. 'A singer, an artist, a trickster – after my daughter's hand! And what is that nonsense you talk about having put the enemy to flight? As if the whole army and all the people had not seen how I myself, riding on my white horse at the head of the cavalry, drove off the Lappatraskian devils! Can you even sit on a horse, you boorish tramp? Guards, lock up this villain! The State Council will investigate his affairs and pass judgment. And arrest the dragon, too! Have it examined by the priests, it must be some kind of witchcraft!'

The next day the State Council examined the case and passed judgment.

His Excellency, the Prime Minister, who was also Minister of Court Etiquette, of Justice and of War, expressed himself thus:

'The matter is highly complicated. In my capacity as Prime Minister I consider that there are serious grounds for hanging the accused in the interest of the state. However, as Minister of Court Etiquette, I consider that in deference to Her Royal Highness the Princess Finissa he should, prior to execution, be raised into the nobility. It is also my duty to consider the case as Minister of Justice, and from that point of view also find that this honour which I have proposed for him is well justified, for it has been established in the course of the trial that the accused – if we set aside the selfishness of his motives and the illegality of his methods – has, next to His Majesty the King, made the most effective contribution to the defence of our country. And finally, as Minister of War I consider that the man merits the State Medal for Valour, eighth class.'

The other members of the State Council agreed. The High Priest, who in his capacity as Minister of Ecclesiastical Affairs had a seat in the Council, added a request that the man should be hanged in secret so that the people would not become agitated. He considered that it might be highly dangerous for religion if the truth were to leak out. And he wished to have it recorded in the minutes that this was an important matter of principle.

The sentence was confirmed by the King and carried out at once. The King accordingly elevated Hannes Elsaffan to the nobility with the title von Drachenflucht, pedigree number 2345, and decorated him with the State Medal for Valour. He was then led out by the guard and hanged in a back yard.

*

Some months later the Princess Finissa, when she went to the river to bathe, attended by her maidens, chanced to find in the rushes a little casket made of bamboo canes daubed together with clay and pitch, and in the casket lay a handsome little baby boy. The Princess adopted the boy as her own child and gave him the name Filiboomboom.

Not long afterwards her wedding with the Duke of Callipasta was celebrated with all due pomp and ceremony, and they lived long and happily together. At times, when she felt depressed, she would take out the bottle with Hannes Elsaffan's soul in it and make it sing:

> It breaks the heart
> When lovers part...

But as years went by the voice began to sound a little cracked.

CHURCHYARD ARABESQUE

(*Kyrkogårdsarabesk,* 1924)

Some years ago now – it was during the War – I was walking with Henning Berger one day in late autumn in a churchyard in Copenhagen. A hundred years ago the place was out in the depths of the country, far from the walls and ditches of the town, but now it is like a great oasis of peace and greenery in the middle of a busy quarter of the city, among department stores, factories and hostels.

We walked slowly along an endless avenue of tall, thin poplars. Now and then we stopped to read the names and inscriptions on the tombstones.

We had been talking about the War. Henning Berger was hoping that Germany would win. I was afraid that Germany would win and not hoping for anything. After a while we began to run out of conversation.

'Look!' he said, pointing to a tombstone at the side of the path, 'look – J. P. Jacobsen! But perhaps it isn't the right one.'

'No, I don't suppose it is. He is sure to be buried at Thisted; that's where he was born and where he died.And this grave is a good hundred years old anyway, you can see that.'

'Yes, of course. What's that relief on it? It reminds me of the Thorvaldsen period.'

It showed a naked young hero with helmet and sword and a ram's fleece over his arm.

'Jason with the Golden Fleece.'

'Oh, so that'll be a tanner buried there.'

We read the inscription. It was a tanner.

We walked on and stopped in front of another grave, also more than a hundred years old. A tall stone with a bronze medallion

136

showing the dead man, a veterinary professor, and under the medallion a large relief of the Diana of Ephesus with her twenty breasts. Rather curious in a Christian churchyard suddenly to come across that old fertility symbol that once gave St Paul such a lot of trouble at Ephesus...

'How on earth does that come to be here?' wondered Berger.

'Goodness knows. Great is the Diana of the Ephesians, but I can't say I'd heard about her services to veterinary science.'

'She was the goddess of the hunt, so perhaps she was also goddess of the hounds,' guessed Berger. 'Maybe that is the explanation. But look at the old fellow in the medallion – do you see who he looks like?'

I saw no resemblance to anybody I knew.

'It is Böök,' he said. 'Can't you see?'

I did what I could to find the likeness between the seventy-year-old veterinary professor and the promising young critic, Dr Böök. But I couldn't.

'You never can see things the same way as I do,' he muttered, dark and gloomy like the autumn weather around us.

(I knew that the spirit of Saul used to descend upon him every time he thought of Böök. It had been like that ever since Böök, who had at one time written quite favourable reports about his books, had suddenly done to death a novel that Berger had had high hopes with. The book had unfortunately appeared too late for Böök to read it in the Christmas rush; he had only managed to look through it a bit, and had guessed the conclusion – but guessed wrong! And then he had condemned the book on account of the feeble, banal ending which he himself had invented. Then, for the sake of consistency, he had continued in the same vein whenever he wrote about Berger.)

'Besides, it's really your fault,' he burst out.

'What do you mean?' I asked.

'It's your fault Böök keeps running me down! You should never have attacked him! Ever since you went for Böök I have been the poor devil that never gets a decent review in *Svenska Dagbladet*! Never! It's as plain as a pikestaff: you never write anything, so he can't get at you. So he goes for your friends instead. We have to pay the costs of your war, and it's damned expensive, I can tell you. Really I ought to send you a bill.'

'Please don't do that, Henning,' I said. 'I should be ruined.'

'Yes, and it would serve you right. That's quite an extravagance you've allowed yourself. Attacking a critic! And a critic in *Svenska Dagbladet* to boot! Anybody would think you had taken leave of your senses!'

'I admit there may be something in what you say. But one can't think of everything, you know. And I never dreamed, when I made that little joke about "Dr Löök" a few years ago, that I would end up having to apologize to you for it...'

'No, but now you've had your little joke and enough is enough! Do you know what I'm going to do now? Well, I shall tell you. I'm going to go right home and write a novel about you, or a column or something or other, and I shall run you down till you're this high, and then I shall send it to *Svenska Dagbladet*! Then we shall see whether or not I can get decent reviews again in that paper!'

'That's an idea,' I said. 'Quite an idea! I shall be delighted to help you. That way we can fix things so that you don't need to send me any bill. And in private we can be just as good friends as ever.'

' – *Of course!* I never dreamed of anything else! Let's play a trick on that devil!'

It had started raining, a fine misty rain at first, and we hardly noticed it, but suddenly it began to tip down. We decided to seek shelter in the gateway of the chapel of rest, as the doors were wide open. A burial was just taking place; the service had started with a hymn and an organ piece. 'Blessed, blessed!' Inside the door there was a cleric, and he gave us each a copy of a printed sheet with the name of the deceased in a black frame and with the texts of the hymns that were to be sung. We sat down in an empty row of pews near the door. I read the name of the deceased: Eva Marta Kristina Ytterquist. Clearly a Swedish name. And one of the wreaths on the coffin had a blue and yellow ribbon. The plain coffin, the meagre wreaths, the tiny handful of mourners, everything seemed to indicate that this was a quiet life that had come to its end. The words of the priest gave the same impression: a humble calling, loyalty in her little world...

The sermon was short, but there were hymns with many long verses, both before and after the sermon. The whole thing lasted the best part of half an hour, the rain passed over, and when the coffin was carried out to the singing of Ingemann's lovely hymn 'Fair is the earth, fine is God's heaven, lovely the pilgrimage of the soul' the weak autumn sunshine entered under the thinning yellow foliage of the trees. And several large tears rolled down Henning's cheek.

'That hymn always has this effect on me,' he said, as if apologizing, to an elderly gentleman who was walking beside us.

(For we naturally went along with the others down to the grave.)

'Yes, it is a lovely hymn,' the man replied in Danish. 'But I can hear that you gentlemen are Swedish. So you have come over here to be at the old lady's funeral? That really is a kind, friendly thought! Perhaps you will say a few words at the graveside?'

Henning Berger became somewhat embarrassed.

'I don't think I can,' he said. 'I haven't prepared anything.'

'Oh, that doesn't matter,' said the kindly little Dane, 'you can always think of something! It is so cold and empty when nobody says anything at the graveside. And I'm sure there's nobody else here who will.'

We had already reached the grave. The priest cast his three scoops of earth upon the coffin in accordance with the ritual, just as in Sweden, and he read out the blessing.

The little man prodded Henning Berger in the side. 'Now,' he said, 'now you must speak!'

I was on tenter-hooks. Henning Berger walked up to the little mound of earth beside the grave, hat in hand, and gazed down for a while upon the coffin, then he lifted his head again and looked out over the little group of mourners. And as he stood up there he looked – as in Herman Vedel's portrait – like an important, dignified prelate.

Then he spoke: 'Eva Marta Kristina! Three names you were given in holy baptism. When I think of Eva I see before me the blossom of your youth. But that is long since withered and gone, and Eva is dead. Peace be with her. And when I think of Marta I see all the labour of your active life. For you worked and cared for many things, and afterwards you were weary and went to your rest. And now Marta, too, is dead.

'But it is different with Kristina! For I know that she lives! As a good Christian you have entered in to the eternal life, Kristina! And we, who still must wander a little longer in this vale of tears, we do not say farewell, but au revoir, until we meet again.'

The speaker was rewarded with tears and warm handshakes when he came down. The priest thanked him and congratulated him like a colleague on the beautiful symbolism which he had found in the three names, which for many people would have seemed so ordinary...

And even I, old sinner as I am, was rather moved.

THE SONATA OF ERRORS

(*Misstagssonaten*, 1925)

At a party given by a Danish family here in Copenhagen recently I heard three short stories which might be described as variations on one and the same theme, and I shall try to repeat them as well as I can.

A sonata generally has three movements, though admittedly they are not usually variations on the same theme. But it pleases me anyway to call this whole thing *The Sonata of Errors*. There is nothing particularly musical about it – nobody is likely to suspect me of lifting it from Beethoven. Another thing, and this is worse – the title doesn't correspond properly to the contents, since I am not concerned with just any errors, but with errors of a quite special kind.

Our host was a wealthy (I believe) and cultured dealer in antiques. Among the guests were his father-in-law, a gentle-mannered, dignified old priest, and then a grey-bearded (but not all that old) Swedish painter, a Norwegian lecturer in philosophy from Oslo University specializing in 'the psychology of the subconscious', and a bank clerk with a sharp, clean-shaven face. The other guests, including myself, may be regarded as supernumerary.

It began when the Norwegian lecturer showed us a letter which he had received that day from one of his colleagues in Oslo, a historian. The strange thing about the letter was the date: 17th November 1425. The year was written quite plainly. There was no question of the sender having written a nine that looked like a four (even if that is possible). And there was nothing in the letter to suggest any joke or mystification.

'The fact of the matter,' said the Norwegian philosopher, 'is

141

quite simply that my old friend for some reason or other had the year 1425 on his mind when he dated this letter. I do not remember what happened in 1425, or whether anything at all happened. But my colleague would know, since he is a historian. Subconsciously he must have been thinking of that year and so he wrote it down, though of course he was quite sure at the time that he was writing 1925. This kind of case is by no means unusual, and I would be glad to hear if anyone else here present can cast any light on the subject from his own experience.'

(Thus we have the theme: now let us proceed to the variations.)

'Yes, as it happens, I have an example,' said the greybearded Swedish painter. 'At one time, some thirty odd years ago, I was passionately in love with a girl. I fell for her so completely I could have married her, though I naturally didn't have any money. I expect it would have cost...

'But since I am in a foreign country I had better first explain that there is a quarter of Stockholm called Östermalm. A hellishly depressing quarter with a lot of straight, depressing streets, and one of them is called Kommendör Street. It is so depressing that I used to think of it as the typical Östermalm street. I come from farming stock in Småland and I didn't like Östermalm, but it so happened that I was renting a room on Kommendör Street – it was facing north-east and could be used as a studio by a poor young devil of an artist.

'One evening I had arranged to meet the girl in Kommendör Street, at a corner not far from my own front door. I had, of course, certain hopes – begging your pardon, pastor...

'But she didn't come. And yet she had promised so definitely! I paced up and down, up and down, for two whole hours. I paced up and down and I wept tears and I swore – begging your pardon, pastor! It was a cold, windy November evening and I had no overcoat. I had pawned that to get money for a bottle of wine and some fancy cakes and grapes and a French pear for the girl. But she didn't come, the little devil – excuse me, pastor!

'Possibly I had a bit of a chill already; the next day I was in bed with a temperature. Pneumonia! Straight off to hospital! Practically kicked the bucket! And when I came out of hospital I read in a paper that the girl was engaged. To a rotten cad that I vaguely knew.

'Six years later we met at a party. I avoided her. But suddenly she was standing next to me in a window-recess and she whispered:

'"Why didn't you come?"

'"Why didn't I come? What do you mean? I was walking up and down Kommendör Street weeping and swearing for two hours! And I got freezing cold and caught pneumonia!"

'"Kommendör Street? But you wrote and asked me to meet you in Östermalm Street! And that is where I was walking up and down in the wind and getting freezing cold, though perhaps not for two hours..."

'You see, the fact is – there is another straight, boring, depressing street in Östermalm, and it really is called Östermalm Street. In my mind I had always thought of Kommendör Street as "the typical Östermalm street". And so I had written Östermalm Street though I meant Kommendör Street! It's strange to think that if I hadn't made that slip my life would have been quite different. Better or worse, who knows? But different!'

The lecturer specializing in the subconscious had taken out a notebook and was hastily writing something down.

'Yes, my dear friends,' said the old priest, 'it really is strange how chance happenings that seem quite trivial can take hold of our lives and fortunes. Once, best part of twenty years ago, I myself had a mishap of a very similar kind, which could well have been the end of my career in the Church. But I am not sure I can tell the story. Ah, well – I am among good friends, who will understand and forgive me.

'I am getting on for eighty years old. But at that time I was only a bit over sixty, and my grandchildren, Sofus and Juliane, who are now sitting in that corner grinning at me, were then only five or six years old and had never been to the Tivoli.

143

'It was a fine Sunday in August in nineteen... let me think... yes, it was 1908. Yes, it was the same year as that unfortunate business with Alberti.

'I was standing in the pulpit in my little church preaching as well as I could. Fortunately, there were not many people in the church. Well – unfortunately, I suppose I should have said. But for me it was fortunate – that time. The text on which I was preaching was Jesus' words on the Cross to the repentant robber: "Verily, verily, I say unto thee, today shalt thou be with me in Paradise."

'We do not know the name of the repentant robber. I recall that I had lately read a novel by a French writer in which the repentant robber was called Gestas. That must be a mistake. In a few of the apocryphal gospels the repentant robber is called Demas and the unrepentant one is called Gestas. But as to what they were really called the proper gospels, which are in the Bible, have nothing to say.

'Well, anyway, that has nothing to do with my story.

'My daughter and her husband – our dear hosts here this evening – and their children Sofus and Juliane were spending that summer in the country up at Rungsted, but that Sunday, it was about the end of August, I was expecting them back in Copenhagen and in the evening we were going to the Tivoli with Sofus, who was six, and Juliane, who was only five. The dear little rascals had never been in the Tivoli before. I remembered the first Tivoli evening of my own childhood, it was a quite unforgettable experience, and I was rejoicing in advance at the way my little grandchildren would enjoy themselves. And these worldly, but really quite innocent thoughts were on my mind – I must, to my shame, admit it – while I was standing in the pulpit interpreting the words of the Gospel. And so it came about that I happened to end my sermon by having Our Lord on the Cross say to the repentant robber: "Verily, verily, I say unto thee, today shalt thou be with me in the Tivoli!"

'As soon as I had said it I *knew* what I had said. And I can tell you without the slightest exaggeration that that was the most dreadful moment in all my life. I didn't dare to look at the congregation. I hid my face in my hands while I stammered and whispered the benediction.

'I scarcely know how I got home. I was an old man – for even in those days I was no youngster – but I took a devious route through back alleys to avoid meeting people and to collect my thoughts. Never in all my life have I felt so lost and miserable. And when I was home I sat down at my desk straight away and wrote to the Ministry of Cultural Affairs. I confessed what I had said in my sermon – it was important to anticipate any reports from my congregation – and I explained the matter as well as I could. And at the end I declared I was willing, if it should be called for, to apply for dismissal from duty with pension.

'After three months – for in the Ministry there is no haste over answering letters – I received a reply. The Minister, who was one of my old friends from university, did me the honour of a reply by his own hand. He wrote that, since not one of the few people in that congregation appeared even to have noticed my little lapsus, let alone taken offence at it, there was no occasion for any kind of action. Actually, I happen to have the letter with me. Here you are! It is the only letter I have ever received from a minister of state.'

('Granddad has always *happened* to have that letter with him for as long as I can remember,' whispered Sofus to Juliane.)

'As we probably all know,' continued the old priest, 'the Christian community, and the Church herself, up to a few centuries ago did not believe in just one devil, but in countless evil spirits which interfered in all the affairs of life, both great and small. And it cannot be denied that this belief has firm support in Holy Scripture; and furthermore, the Church has never repudiated that view – it has merely slipped out of Christian preaching, as if by itself, in more recent times. But I for my part have seen and heard and experienced a good many things which prevent me from rejecting that teaching. How, otherwise, are we to explain the phenomenon of "speaking with tongues"? It has happened many times, and it happened already in St Paul's time, that a man who was speaking with tongues, when "the spirit" had seized him, uttered the most terrible blasphemies and cursed Our Lord Jesus Christ – and afterwards had not the least idea what he had said. Must not that "spirit" have been an evil spirit? And what about my own case? Must it not have been a little trouble-making devil – a devil of mischief – that prompted me to say something I never thought nor meant and that I never dreamed I would be able to say from a pulpit?'

'Yes, pastor,' said the Norwegian lecturer, 'I really don't know what to say about it. The evil spirits which at one time were believed to cause diseases have in modern medical science taken on a kind of concrete form in the shape of bacteria. But we have not yet found anything corresponding to that in the science of psychology. But who knows? Perhaps that will come!'

'Your health, professor!' said the Swedish painter. 'And yours, pastor! And let us drink the health of that trouble-making little devil! Here's to that devil of mischief!'

I had thought for some time that I could tell from the face of the clean-shaven banker with the sharp features that he, too, had something to contribute – another variation on the theme. And I was quite right.

'Unfortunately,' he began with a thin but penetrating voice, 'unfortunately I am not an artist, like our honoured guest from Sweden, nor am I a professional psychologist like our Norwegian brother, and I am not an eminent preacher like our distinguished old friend. I am just an ordinary bank clerk. But once, not so many years ago, I too experienced – though only as an accessory and a witness – an error of exactly the kind we are talking about. Quite a serious error, too, and not least from a banker's point of view.

'But, as I have said, I was not myself the one that made the mistake; and that is why I don't really know where to begin. Our Swedish and Norwegian guests have presumably never heard of the writer Marius Krebs...'

'Oh yes!' said the Swedish painter. 'I have even read one of his books. But that was at least thirty years ago.'

'Really? Well, he was quite a good writer in his day. He just happened to live twenty or thirty years too long. He had a few plays produced at the Royal Theatre at the beginning of the eighties. And he wrote three or four books which were read and discussed and even bought. In later years he wrote other books which were neither read nor bought and consequently were not discussed. And so he grew old and died in poverty and want ten years or so ago, as completely forgotten as if he had never lived.

'But about a week before he died he had a letter from the bank where I have a rather junior appointment. In the letter there was a draft for 3,730 crowns and a short note from the bank stating that the sum cabled from such-and-such a bank in New York was to be paid to the writer Marius Krebs of 24 Forhaabningsholms Allé.

'What did he think when that letter came? I cannot imagine. Perhaps he had a son or daughter in America. Or a grandson or granddaughter. Perhaps he thought that one of them might possibly have hit on the kind idea of sending him a thousand dollars. Or else – surely it was possible? – some American publisher was sending him that staggering sum as a courtesy honorarium for the translation rights of one of his books which the publisher had made a fortune with... Well, heaven knows what he thought! I can just picture him as he rubbed his bald head and tugged at his thin white beard. However it might be, he put on his Sunday suit and took a taxi, which he had no money to pay for, and drove to the bank.

'It was my counter at the bank that he came to collect his money from. I took the draft and examined it back and front. It was in order. And I had known Marius Krebs by sight for many years – he was an old Copenhagen character – and so there was no need of any proof of identity. I counted out the money. Marius Krebs had only to pick it up and stuff it into his wallet, if he had one, and then to leave.

'But that is not what he did. Instead, he asked:

'"Excuse an old man's curiosity, sir. But tell me, where does this money come from?"

'I had just returned to duty that day after several weeks'

holiday which I had spent in Norway. I therefore knew nothing about it and I had not seen the cable from New York.

'"I am afraid I cannot say," I replied. "But it must have been in the letter from the bank which you had with the draft." "Yes," he said. "It says 'by cable' – from a bank in New York that I have never heard of. But I would like to know who it is that is sending me the money. Does it say in the cable, perhaps?"

'He showed me the notification from the bank. It was one of our usual printed letters, on which the name and the amount had been written in. Looking at the words in ink, I recognized at once Miss Iversen's handwriting.

'"Miss Iversen," I said, "would you show us that cable from New York about a payment of 1,000 dollars to Mr Marius Krebs, please? Mr Krebs would like to see it."

'Miss Iversen stared at me with big, frightened eyes.

'"To... to Mr Marius Krebs?"

'"That's right!"

'Her whole face went red and her hands shook as she fumbled among the papers in the file where the cable ought to be.

'"I can't find it," she whispered.

'Suddenly she burst into tears and ran away.

'As we discovered later, she ran and hid in... well, in the only place where a girl can hide for a while when she is in a desperate tight corner.

'I looked through the file where the cable should have been myself. True enough, it wasn't there. Instead I found a cable from the New York bank authorizing payment of 1,000 dollars to Mr Marius Kristensen. A well-known film writer. Now it was my turn to feel a strong urge to run away and hide. Personally, of course, I had nothing to reproach myself with, but I still felt dreadfully ashamed. On the bank's account. One always feels some degree of solidarity with an institution where one has worked for many years. And an error of the kind that had clearly arisen in this case simply cannot occur in a bank.

'And how in the world was I to explain the situation to Mr Marius Krebs? I asked him to take a seat while we looked for the cable. It would soon turn up, I lied.

'Marius Krebs trotted across to a bench and sat down. His trusting, child-like eyes stared, perhaps in bewilderment, at the cubist wall-paintings in the bank chamber. Our bank always did pride itself on keeping abreast of the times.

'I sent a young lady to look for Miss Iversen. Finally she appeared, pale and tear-stained. I showed her the notification from the bank which she had filled in – with the name of Marius Krebs – and the cable from New York with Marius Kristensen's name. She explained as well as she could. She had lately, by sheer chance, been reading an old book by Marius Krebs and it had made a deep impression on her. And so, without knowing what she was doing, she had written Krebs instead of Kristensen.

'Mr Marius Krebs made his way to the counter. "Excuse me," he said, "but I have a taxi waiting outside. It has been waiting now for over half an hour. That is going to be expensive. And the only money I have is what I am going to draw with this draft... What about the cable? Has it been found yet?"

'"Well, yes, in a way, Mr Krebs," I replied. "But... the fact is, one of our young lady assistants has made a most distressing and unfortunate mistake."

'I showed him the cable and repeated Miss Iversen's explanation. And as to the taxi, I asked him to permit a young man on our staff, who could be spared for the moment, to travel home with him and pay the driver.

'I had naturally been afraid that the old man would have a terrible shock. But instead he took it with a sense of humour.

'"I thought something must be wrong," he said. "I have never been lucky with money. But would you mind if I ask which of my books it was that the young lady had been reading? Would it be *Margrete Hill* by any chance?"

'"Yes, Mr Krebs, that was the book,", sobbed Miss Iversen.

'The old writer's face lit up. "Really?" he said, "was it really?"

'And the next day Miss Iversen received a copy of *Margrete*

Hill with the author's dedication and a little bouquet of tall daisies and bluebells.

'About a week after that I saw a little notice in *Politiken* that the writer Marius Krebs was dead. Well, we all have to die, and I don't suppose that episode had anything to do with it. But Miss Iversen thought otherwise. She dressed in black for a whole month, and for years afterwards she always went to his grave on the anniversary of his death with a little bouquet of tall daisies and bluebells.'

There was a little pause.

'Yes,' said the Swedish painter, 'that is the way things can happen sometimes. Mostly in little matters, of course – but what are little matters and what are big ones? And who knows if, perhaps, Our Lord, when He created this world, really intended something quite different?'

THE STOVE THAT WASN'T REAL

(Den overkliga kakelugnen, 1931)

In the autumn evenings when the first fires were lit my father
sometimes used to amuse us children, and perhaps himself as
well, by playing with the fire. When the flames had burnt down
he would build a castle in the embers with an empty cigar-case
and a few match-boxes, and a wad of thick cartridge-paper
would make a tower. For a long time the whole splendid
construction would stand smouldering gently before the fire
really took hold. But then! Nero could hardly have derived
more joy from the burning of Rome that I had from these
improvised little fires in the autumn evenings. A serious
educationist would perhaps disapprove of this kind of pleasure:
the child must get the idea that a grand blaze was the finest
thing in the world, and I have often in later years been surprised
at this imaginative streak in my father, who was otherwise
always so proper and respectable. And I was, in fact, not a little
put out when I heard one morning that the German Church had
burnt down during the night while I was asleep. But fortunately
I was fully compensated soon afterwards by seeing the big fire
at the Steam Mill.* I was walking with my father through the
old town one winter evening when we saw a bright glow in the
sky. My father had the keys to his office in the Treasury, in the
south wing of the old Kungshus Building on Riddarholm
Island; he took me there with him and we watched the big fire,

---

* Translator's note: Stockholm's first steam-driven flour mill burned down in
1878. The building stood on the waterfront on the site of the present Town Hall,
and the conspicuous blaze was reflected in the dark waters. Prince Eugene
produced a painting of the fire.

the finest blaze Stockholm has had in my time, as we looked out from the big, round room in the tower, the conference room, which had been a council room in Frederick I's time. Great flocks of pigeons, which the fire had made homeless, were flying in wide circles over the blaze, and the sharp red light they reflected made them look like flickering sparks thrown up from the fire.

After that I suppose I was no longer quite so impressed with our little fires in the tiled stove at home. But, anyway, it was playing with the fire and the dying embers like this on autumn evenings that gave me my first childhood impressions of what we used to call 'atmosphere' – a word that now, perhaps, has been cheapened by too much use. And so I developed a rather special affection for the old stove.

And that is why it came as something of a shock to me when, some years later, at the age of sixteen, I was initiated to the school of philosophy which was then called 'pure idealism' (no doubt it still is so called in the history of philosophy) and I was led by this to doubt the very existence of the stove.

A young relative, the son of somebody who had been married to a cousin of my father's (both the parents were dead) came to stay with us. He was five or six years older than me and a student at Uppsala, and since he lived in a remote place in the country I had never met him before. His name was Albert. The difference in rank and age between a student and a schoolboy is far greater than between a professor and a student. I therefore felt deeply flattered when Albert spoke to me as to an equal and honoured me with long talks about deep philosophical questions. He explained to me that the stove, in which a freshly-lit birch-wood fire was blazing away, only existed 'within me', that is to say in my mind.

'But doesn't it also exist within you?' I asked, 'in *your* mind?'

'Certainly,' he said. 'For me it exists *only* within me, just as for you it exists *only* within you.'

'But for me, surely, it can't exist *only* within me, because I know that it also exists within you, and within mother and father, and within Lotta who lit the fire.'

'For you,' answered Albert, 'I exist only within you, in your own mind. And it is just the same with your mother and father and Lotta the maid. What you know or think you know about my mind or other people's minds, all that really exists only in your own.'

And he explained at length how everything which we call the external world, the objects around us, things and people and animals, the sun and the moon, the stars and the earth, were nothing more than the contents of our own minds. It is not possible to know anything at all about whatever exists outside our minds – if anything exists at all. But learning cannot concern itself with that which it is impossible to know, and for philosophy, which is the highest kind of learning, the contents of the mind must therefore be the only reality. Outside of our mind there is no reality to be found, or even imagined, for in the very moment when I imagine something, that 'something' already exists in my mind.

I gave the matter a little thought. His line of argument struck me as perfectly correct and at the same time quite crazy. But I could not sort out in a hurry what was correct about it and what was crazy.

'Father,' I said, 'how old would you say this house is?'

'Let me think,' said my father. 'It was built when I was at secondary school. So it must be something like forty years old.'

'So the man who made the stove must be dead by this time, otherwise we could ask him. The stove must have existed in his mind before he constructed it: he knew what it was going to be like. At any rate it is possible that it did not turn out exactly as he had conceived it in the first place. And in that case he must have been forced to alter the idea of the stove in his mind as he was working on it. How are you going to account for that if you will not allow that something from a reality outside his mind caused him to alter the idea of the stove that was in his mind? Besides, the man who made the stove surely had a much clearer idea than we have about how the stove is constructed internally: could that perhaps be because he was working with a reality that is now known to us?'

I thought, of course, that I was handling this rather well. But Albert was not of the same opinion.

'I don't know whether you have done any logic at school,' he said. 'If you have then you may remember that there is a kind of error called the 'circular argument'. It consists of presupposing what you are trying to prove. You base your whole argument on the assumption that there is a reality outside your mind, and in that way you think you have proved its existence. The reality of the stove does at least to some extent have the appearance in its favour, since you can see it with your own eyes at this moment – and so you try to prove its reality by means of the stove-maker's reality, even though you have probably never in all your life seen a stove-maker.'

'But tell me, Albert,' said my father, 'do you not yourself, in ordinary matters, when it is not a question of philosophy, make a certain distinction between real and not real?'

'That is a practical necessity,' replied Albert. 'Our consciousness is by nature so constituted that we necessarily have to regard some things as real and some other things as not real. But it does not follow from that that any such difference exists in reality.'

'I thought you said just now,' I resumed, 'that the contents of our mind are the only true reality. But now you concede that there is in our mind a difference between real and not real. Our mind presumably has some reason for making that distinction. I had a certain idea of you before I had seen you. I knew you were a student. I also have an old photograph of you where you are a little boy with short trousers and curly hair. In a dark corner of my mind I therefore imagined you at one time as a very small student with short trousers and curly hair. But now that I have met you I have been compelled to abandon the picture of you that was in my mind: you are not short, but on the contrary rather tall, and you do not have short trousers or curly hair. What is it that has forced me to abandon my old image of you and replace it with a new one? Could it not possibly be my coming into contact with a reality that existed outside my own mind before it entered into it?'

I do not recall what Albert said to that, but I expect it was something very profound, and we continued our dispute for a long time without coming to any conclusion. I never saw him again; some years after that he died as a result of an accident. If he had lived he might well have one day become the great philosopher which our country, unfortunately, has never yet produced.

King Gustav Vasa's farewell speech to the Estates is, as we know, not an entirely dependable verbatim record, and I also cannot be absolutely sure that my second cousin Albert and I on that occasion said in just those words everything that is written down in this little philosophical dialogue – which in any case is just about as foolish as some of the dialogues of Plato.

HJALMAR SÖDERBERG

Martin Birck's Youth

(translated by Tom Ellett)

Hjalmar Söderberg's partly autobiographical second novel was originally published in 1901, and traces the development of the title character from a seemingly idyllic Stockholm childhood to maturity as a thirty-year-old man, an introspective outsider, critical of society, constantly searching for the truth but going through a gradual process of disillusionment. He dreams of being a poet, but is too melancholic to break free from his modest bureaucratic career, and slowly drifts towards nihilism and aestheticism.

Martin Birck's Youth is a book rich in *fin-de-siècle* themes: melancholy, eroticism and decadence abound. The Stockholm depicted here is a haunting city of shadows and snowstorms, suppressed passion and loneliness. The conflict between dreams and reality which occurs in so many novels of the period is central to the novel, and its preoccupation with issues of free will, determinism and morality prefigures Söderberg's next novel, the highly acclaimed *Doctor Glas* (in which Martin Birck makes a cameo appearance).

ISBN 978 1 870041 59 3
UK £8.95
(paperback, 152 pages)

HJALMAR BERGMAN

Memoirs of a Dead Man

(translated by Neil Smith)

'Not everyone who lives is alive; nor is death a portal that only opens in one direction'

Hjalmar Bergman (1883-1931) is widely regarded as one of the foremost Swedish novelists of the twentieth century. *Memoirs of a Dead Man*, first published in 1918, follows the efforts of Jan Arnberg, the 'dead man' of the title (although there are numerous other candidates worthy of the description among Bergman's gallery of characters), to escape the curse that has bound the fate of his family to that of the Arnfelts for generations.

The earlier efforts of Jan's father to break free of the curse by moving to America founder in a biting parody of consumer society and advertising slogans. Jan's own story culminates when he has to flee a small-town scandal in Sweden and ends up in a symbolic kingdom of death in Hamburg, a mixture of casino and high-class brothel, where the family curse is played out once more, and where he comes to realize that abdication from free will is his only option.

Although apparently realistic to begin with, Bergman's novel shifts towards a theatrical, dreamlike world of repetitions and refractions in which the fates of his characters are predetermined and acted out in a macabre mixture of comedy and nightmare. Characters presumed dead manifest themselves in incidental roles throughout the novel, casting a foreboding light on the almost biblical nature of the family curse.

ISBN 978 1 870041 65 2
UK £10.95
(paperback, 352 pages)

AUGUST STRINDBERG

Tschandala

(translated by Peter Graves)

August Strindberg's novella *Tschandala* was written in the autumn of 1888, the same year as the dramas *Miss Julie* and *Creditors*. The setting is historical: the time is the 1690s and the location is Skåne, the southern province that Sweden annexed from Denmark in 1658. A Swedish academic from the University of Lund, Andreas Törner, rents rooms for the summer with his family in a dilapidated manor house, owned by an eccentric baroness and managed a gipsy named Jensen. Although puzzled by the peculiarities of the people and environment, initially Törner enjoys a good relationship with the people of the house, but he is drawn into conflict with the Jensen, whom he suspects of lies, criminality and incompetence. The conflict intensifies, culminating in a struggle for survival between the two men. The atmosphere and setting of the story are thoroughly Gothic: the ruinous castle, mystery and suspense, inexplicable events, strange aristocrats and gipsies, baying hounds, and unexplained noises. All of this is, however, interwoven with ideas drawn from Nietzsche and Social Darwinism.

ISBN 978 1 870041 71 3
UK £8.95
(paperback, 136 pages)

AUGUST STRINDBERG
The Red Room

(translated by Peter Graves)

August Strindberg (1849-1912) is best known outside Sweden as a dramatist, but he was also a prolific writer of novels, short stories, essays, journalism and poetry – as well as a notable artist and photographer. Although he spent many years abroad, Strindberg was born, grew up and died in Stockholm and *The Red Room* is perhaps the quintessential Stockholm novel. A satire of the rapidly changing society of the 1870s, it was Strindberg's first novel and marked his literary breakthrough: it offers, he said, 'a panorama of a society I don't love and which has never loved me'. It contains some of the great set-piece scenes in Swedish literature, a gallery of unforgettable caricatures in the spirit of Dickens, humour, pathos and satirical targets as apt now as they were then. *The Red Room* is often called Sweden's first modern novel, and it remains modern almost a century and a half later.

'In the opening chapter, with its famous bird's-eye view of Stockholm, Strindberg's vivid prose sparkles with energy and invention. The hero of the novel, the young and idealistic Arvid Falk, resigns from the Civil Service in disgust at the corruption he sees everywhere in the Establishment. He wants to become a writer and joins a group of bohemian artists, but struggles to free himself from his own prim and puritan inclinations. [...] As so often in Strindberg, it is the tension between irreconcilable opposites that provides the narrative energy.'
      Ulf Dantanus, *1001 Books You Must Read Before You Die*

ISBN 978 1 870041 82 9
UK £9.95
(paperback, 315 pages)

RUNAR SCHILDT

The Meat-Grinder and Other Stories

(translated by Martin and Anna-Lisa Murrell)

Runar Schildt (1888-1925) is one of the major figures of Finland-Swedish literature, and one of Finland's finest short-story writers. His precisely observed depictions of Helsingfors life in the early decades of the twentieth century, his acute sense of irony and delicately drawn characters place him firmly among the foremost exponents of the European short story.

This anthology brings together stories from different stages of Schildt's career for the first time in English. His early writing depicts the decadence and heady social whirl of upper-class Helsingfors in the years preceding the Finnish Civil War of 1918. 'The Weaker One', regarded by many to be Schildt's masterpiece, is a particularly sharply drawn story of adultery and deception.

ISBN 978 1 870041 56 0
UK £9.95
(paperback, 318 pages)

For further information, or to request a catalogue, contact:
Norvik Press, Department of Scandinavian Studies, University College London,
Gower Street, London WC1E 6BT, England
e-mail: norvik.press@ucl.ac.uk

Website: www.norvikpess.com

Lightning Source UK Ltd.
Milton Keynes UK
UKHW021326040119
334924UK00003B/104/P